'I just don't understand you.'

Zara took an unsteady breath. 'Do you want to?'

'Yes,' he said after a long moment. 'I think I do. As soon as I decide what kind of person you are you do something that alters my whole way of thinking.'

'Does that bother you?' Zara moved a little nearer, her hand on the rail, her bare shoulders caressed by the glow of the lamp.

'Yes, it bothers me,' Thor said harshly.

STORMY
VOYAGE

BY

SALLY WENTWORTH

MILLS & BOON LIMITED
ETON HOUSE   18-24 PARADISE ROAD
RICHMOND   SURREY   TW9 1SR

*First published in Great Britain 1992
by Mills & Boon Limited*

© Sally Wentworth 1992

*Australian copyright 1992
Philippine copyright 1992
This edition 1992*

ISBN 0 263 77466 X

*Set in Times Roman 10 on 12 pt.
01-9203-54491 C*

Made and printed in Great Britain

CHAPTER ONE

THE half-dozen electric fans that whirred from the ceiling of the nightclub did little except stir air thick with tobacco smoke and the smell of highly spiced food. They certainly didn't cool a temperature that must have been well over a hundred degrees. As Zara danced she could feel the sweat soaking into her costume. Not that there was much to the costume—just some feathers and three lots of sequins sewn strategically on to a body-stocking. And if Marcel had had his way there would only have been one lot instead of three. But there was no way that Zara was going to bare her boobs to the ogling eyes of the native Arabs and visiting sailors who frequented the club, even though Maxine, the lead dancer and an ex Paris Follies girl, did so without a qualm. But then, Maxine had been a dancer for a long time and she had Marcel to protect her; Zara was alone and fresh out of England—and definitely wishing that she was back there.

The dance came to an end and the five girls—although Maxine was nearing forty and could hardly be called a girl—ran off to change their costumes while Marcel took their place to sing an old ballad in his phoney French accent. Thankfully the next number was the last, their big finale. It was called 'Carnival' and for it they wore tall head-dresses, lots more sequins and spreading trains of brightly coloured feathers which clipped round their waists. The costumes had originally been made for the Follies, and Maxine had bought them through a friend a couple of years ago. Since then they had been used for

5

four shows a day, six days a week, passing from girl to girl as the dancers changed and from nightclub to nightclub as the seasons changed. By now they were looking exceedingly tatty, like birds of paradise which had grown old and bald.

There was little applause when they came running back on, the professional smiles fixed on their faces. This audience was either too jaded or too drunk to show any enthusiasm; they came to ogle more than to be entertained. The girls went into their routine and while Zara danced she tried not to think of the eyes watching her, or of what went on in the minds behind the eyes. The recorded music rose to its big crescendo as they high-kicked and Marcel and Maxine sang, their voices lower than they should have been for the song. But then, as they often said, what was the point of straining your voice for that audience? They all ran off, came back to take an uncalled-for bow, and that was it for the night at last. Or rather for the morning, because the last show didn't finish until three-thirty.

There was the usual rush to change—into trousers and a shirt for Zara and Danielle, the French girl she shared a room with, but two of the other girls put on evening dresses and went back into the club to mingle with the customers. How closely they mingled Zara didn't ask, but they always had more money to spend than they earned as wages.

There was a rap on the door and Marcel's voice demanding impatiently, 'Are you ready?'

It was part of the deal that he walked them back to their hotel every night, but he did so with a bad grace, wanting to get back to the club and take advantage of any free drinks he was offered. But there was no way that the two girls would walk unescorted through the streets of Oran at that time of night.

He hurried them out of the rear door of the club, giving them no time to cream off the stage make-up, let alone use the shower. The fresh air felt so good after the stuffy atmosphere. Zara took in several deep breaths and smelt a faint tang of the sea, making her heart fill with a strange but fierce longing that she couldn't define. Perhaps it was a wanderlust deep within her soul—or perhaps it was just for some clean air, she thought with an inward giggle at this romantic flight of fancy.

Their hotel was in a street of tall old buildings within sight of the waterfront, which, for Zara, was its only advantage. It was decrepit, noisy, and smelly, but their room near the top of the hotel had a most marvellous view out over the harbour which fascinated Zara. Every day when she awoke she would sit in a chair by the window, her elbows on the sill, and watch the constantly changing scene. Ships loading or unloading under the hot sun, on their way to Greece or Turkey, or through the Suez Canal and into the Red Sea. They were nearly all cargo ships—there was nothing here to attract cruise liners to stop. Which was a great pity, Zara thought with a sigh; if she could have got a job on a cruise liner she would have left Oran like a shot.

Danielle was, as always, still asleep when Zara awoke the next day. The French girl lay on her back, her dyed blonde hair spread over the pillow, her mouth parted, her breathing heavy and noisy. When they had first shared the room Zara had crept about, afraid of waking the other girl, but two months of intimacy had taught her that nothing would waken Danielle until she came to naturally. She had even slept through an electric storm that had done a lot of damage to the town and was the

worst Zara had ever experienced, waking at her usual
time and wanting to know what all the fuss was about.

Going over to the window, Zara pushed open the
peeling shutters and let the midday sun burst into the
room with all the noise of the busy street and the
harbour. The water near the docks was almost hidden
by the amount of shipping, but that which showed was
oily and thick with floating rubbish, pieces of broken
crates and innumerable drink cans. But out beyond the
ships, where the great harbour met the open sea, the sun
coruscated off the waves so sharply that it hurt her eyes.
There were several ships out at sea, the smoke rising from
their funnels in black columns that drifted slowly away.
A movement far off on the left horizon caught her eye
and as Zara watched she gradually discerned the outline
of an old-fashioned sailing ship, beating up towards the
harbour. It came nearer under a cloud of white sails that
billowed in the breeze, tall, sleek and beautiful. As it
approached the harbour mouth most of the sails were
lowered to reveal three tall masts, and then the ship came
in the rest of the way under power.

Zara sighed, seized by a fit of nostalgia, and continued to watch as the ship was skilfully steered between
the mass of boats and berthed some distance from the
main loading docks.

Behind her Danielle stirred. The two girls showered
and dressed and went into the town for lunch; they
weren't allowed to cook anything in their room, but this
hardly mattered as one of the few perks they had was a
free meal at the nightclub every evening. After lunch
Danielle went off to visit some French-Algerian friends
who lived locally. Zara did a little essential shopping—
she didn't have any money to fritter away as she was
saving up for her fare back to England—then, at a loose

end, she strolled down to the harbour and walked round to where she could see the sailing ship more clearly.

It was called *Spirit of the Wind*. Hot from her walk, Zara leaned against the harbour wall and looked down at the ship moored at the wharf below. There seemed to be a great deal of activity on the ship's deck. An ambulance was drawn up alongside and presently a man on a stretcher was carried down the gangplank, put in the ambulance, and driven away. The members of the crew lined the side to watch it go, but were almost immediately called back to work by a tall man in a seaman's hat and jacket, the only member of the crew to wear even a semblance of a uniform; most of the men wore just shorts on their suntanned bodies. A battered taxi drove along the wharf and the tall man, who seemed to be in charge, got into it and was driven away. Zara expected to see the work on the deck immediately slow down, but another man, shorter and with a bushy red beard, seemed to take over command and the crew worked as hard as before, doing mysterious things with the sails and making a human chain to pass empty boxes and crates down on to the wharf.

One of the crew, a young man who looked to be in his early twenties and who wasn't as brown as the rest, noticed her watching and gave her a cheeky wave. Zara hesitated for a moment but then returned the wave before turning away and walking back through the town. She attracted many eyes as she walked, one of the few blondes among so many olive-skinned dark-haired women. And one of the few women who walked alone. A couple of times she'd been approached by men in the harbour, which was why she seldom went there any more—a shame because she enjoyed all the bustle. But she wasn't afraid to walk in the smarter shopping areas of the town in daylight, although she wouldn't even go there alone at night.

Danielle was waiting for her at the usual place and they walked back to the hotel together before going on to the nightclub. That night was much as others; they did the first two shows to a half-empty room, the place not filling up until gone eleven. During the third show a party of men she hadn't seen before, about six of them, were sitting on her side of the club and near enough for her to go up to in the part of the act where the girls had to pretend to flirt with members of the audience. A necessary evil, unfortunately. You had to be careful during this not to pick anyone who was at all drunk as it was amazing where their hands could reach in just a few seconds. More than one of the girls had come away with a few feathers missing.

Going up to the table, Zara gave her professionally bright smile and said, *'Bonjour, chéri,'* to the nearest man. He grinned back but another voice called, 'Hello. Remember me?' in English, and she recognised the young deck-hand from the sailing ship.

'You're English?' She gave him a proper smile. 'So am I.'

And then she swung gracefully away and moved to the next table where a hawk-nosed Arab stripped her with hungry eyes. Zara got away from him fast and ran back to go on with the dance.

The crew were still there for the next show and joined in when the girls did their Cockney routine, singing the old London songs with more enthusiasm than skill.

When the show was over the nightclub-owner spoke to Marcel, who banged on the dressing-room door while they were changing. 'A man in the audience wants Zara to have a drink with him.'

It was by no means an unusual request for one or other of the girls. Zara went to the door and opened it a few inches. 'Who is it?' she asked, thinking it might be the young crewman.

But Marcel said persuasively, 'A very important local man.'

Zara already knew what her answer would be, but asked curiously, 'Where is he sitting?'

'On the left, at the second table along near the dance-floor.'

She remembered the hawk-faced Arab and shuddered. 'You know my rule: I don't drink with the customers.'

'Well, this time you've got to,' Marcel said forcibly, his attitude changing completely. 'The owner wants to keep in with him.'

'Too bad; I came here to dance, not to act as a hostess to the customers. Ask Maria or Elaine,' she suggested.

'He doesn't want Maria or Elaine; he asked for you.'

'Then tell him no.'

Zara went to close the door but Marcel stuck his foot in it. 'If you don't go and have a drink with him he could make things unpleasant for the owner. And then the owner could make things even more unpleasant for us. Do you want to get us fired? He's only asking you to have a drink, for heaven's sake.'

'No,' Zara said firmly, knowing that if she had a drink with the man he would expect much more. 'And you'd better move your foot if you don't want it squashed.'

Marcel glowered at her angrily. 'I'm getting rid of you as soon as I can get a replacement. I don't want girls who can't be pleasant to the customers.'

Zara glared back. 'I'm not surprised—pimping is right up your street.' And she slammed the door, making him skip back out of the way.

He got his own back by refusing to walk them home until he was ready to go, so she and Danielle had to spend some of their hard-earned money on a taxi. As the taxi pulled away a big car fell in behind them and followed them all the way back to the hotel. Zara noticed and watched it uneasily, growing alarmed when it stopped behind them. 'You pay,' she said urgently to Danielle. 'I'm going to run in.'

Pushing open the taxi door, she ran across the pavement and into the entrance, ignoring a shout from the car. The hotel-owner was at the desk, a massively big Frenchman who had been invalided out of the army after hurting his leg in an accident some years ago. He looked up when she ran in. 'Trouble?'

'A car followed us.'

He limped out from behind the desk, his bulk a welcome protection.

Danielle came through the entrance door. 'It's the Arab from the nightclub; he wants to talk to you.'

'No,' Zara said very definitely.

'Leave him to me; I'll tell him.' The proprietor went out of the door and the two girls ran up to their room.

'I'm sorry I left you to face him,' Zara apologised when they were safely inside.

Danielle shrugged. 'You should have talked to him. Now you have intrigued him and he will make a great nuisance of himself until he gets what he wants.'

'Well, if he wants me then the answer will always be no,' Zara said forcefully.

Danielle gave a short laugh. 'Men like that always get what they want.' She gave an open-mouthed yawn. 'I'm tired. Goodnight.' And she got into bed without bothering to remove her make-up.

Zara creamed off her own make-up and showered, then turned off the light before going over to the window to close the shutters. It was still dark, too early for the dawn, but the city and harbour were quiet for once, the ships in darkness except for a few lights on gangways and at the masts. Looking over the harbour to where the *Spirit of the Wind* was moored, Zara thought she could make out the riding lights on its masts. She wondered how long it was staying in Oran, whether it would be gone when she awoke the next day.

It was still there; it was the first thing she looked for when she pushed open the shutters, and Zara felt an absurd sense of pleasure to see the ship still tied to the wharf. Dressing quickly, she decided to go and have another look at it after she'd done her shopping; she had a pair of dancing shoes to collect from the menders.

The incident the night before had been unpleasant, but Zara wouldn't have thought of it again if, when she went downstairs, the proprietor hadn't called her over and said, 'The man who followed you last night—he left this for you.' And he held out a small jeweller's box.

Zara shook her head. 'I don't want anything from him. Didn't you tell him I wasn't interested?'

Instead of answering the proprietor said gruffly, 'His name is Ali Messaad. He is a local landowner and he has great power here in Oran.'

She stared at him, realising that he would not—or could not—protect her, and felt suddenly trapped. Then she shook off the mood; there were hundreds of other hotels...she could always move. 'I don't want it. Send it back to him.'

'I was told to show it to you.' And he opened the box to display a pair of gold filigree earrings, the type that was very common in North Africa, although these were larger and more ornate than most that she'd seen.

Again she shook her head. 'Send them back. Tell him I'm not interested.'

Going quickly outside, she paused to put on her sunglasses and noticed that a white-robed Arab in a doorway opposite straightened up from where he'd been slouching in the shade. Turning towards the main shopping centre, Zara began to walk briskly along, glancing in the windows as she went. She stopped to look in one window more closely—and saw in its reflection that the Arab was following her. Her heart began to thump uneasily, but the man wasn't Ali Messaad. He had been in western dress and had looked far too proud and arrogant to put on robes and follow her round the streets. But he could easily employ someone to do so.

The thought made her turn and walk on, wondering what to do. Reaching the shoe shop, she went in but had to wait while the cobbler carried out a spirited argument with a woman customer. Her own transaction was carried out quite quickly, and Zara went back out into the sun, looking round to see if the Arab was still there. At first she didn't see him, but then noticed him further along the road, standing at the kerb, gesticulating at a big black limousine that was approaching him and pointing back towards the shop. It didn't take a great deal of intelligence to guess who was in the limousine. Ducking down a side-alley, Zara ran to the street that lay parallel with the one she'd been in and jumped on to a bus going back towards her hotel and the harbour, pushing her way inside until she was hidden by the other passengers.

For the first time she began to feel really uneasy. Whoever this man, Ali Messaad, was, he obviously didn't like taking no for an answer. She stayed on the bus till it reached the far side of the harbour and then jumped off just as it was about to pull away from the stop, and ran down a street crowded with market stalls. Confident that she'd shaken off anyone trying to follow her, Zara instinctively headed for the sailing ship. There was far less activity on it today. At first she thought the deck was deserted, but then she noticed two members of the crew stretched out, sunbathing, and one of them, from his paler skin, was the young deck-hand she had seen yesterday.

Going down to the wharf, Zara called out, 'Ahoy, there.'

A head bobbed up over the rail. 'Hello.' It was the young crewman, his voice full of astonished pleasure at the sight of her. 'Hang on, I'll be right there.'

He joined her only a couple of minutes later, wearing frayed denim shorts and a T-shirt with the name of the ship emblazoned on it.

'Hello,' he said again.

'Hi. I came to take a closer look at the boat.'

He pulled a comical face. 'And there was I thinking it was me you wanted to meet.' But then he grinned. 'I should have known; it attracts everyone.' He gestured towards the gangplank. 'Come aboard, then.'

But Zara hung back. 'Are you sure it's all right?'

'Yes, you've come at a good time. There's only me and Mack aboard at the moment. The others have gone to the hospital to visit the cook. He's been taken ill.'

Remembering the man she'd seen taken off in an ambulance, Zara said, 'What happened to him?' as she went up the gangplank.

'He's got appendicitis. That's why we came into port here. We weren't going to, but then he got ill and the skipper made for Oran fast. It was touch and go but we made it,' he added with pride in his voice. 'She's a fine ship.'

'She looks it,' Zara agreed, looking round her.

'I'll show you round. My name's Tony, by the way.'

'I'm Zara.'

He took her round the boat with the obvious enthusiasm of a new boy, telling her lots of technical stuff about the sails that she didn't understand, and he had probably only recently learnt himself from the way he recited them parrot-fashion. But he was a nice boy and obviously pleased to have a girl to show off to. He introduced her to the other crewman, who lifted a bored hand in acknowledgement, and then took her below to show her the galley and the crew's quarters. The accommodation seemed very cramped, only the captain and the cook each having a cabin to themselves; the others all slept in tiered bunks, three to a cabin, although in each there was a spare bunk, piled high with clothes and other gear belonging to the sailors. There were eight of them in the crew, Tony told her, including the man who had been taken to hospital.

'How long will you be here?' Zara asked him.

He shrugged. 'Not long. We shouldn't really be here at all.'

'Aren't you going to wait until your cook is better?'

Tony shook his head. 'We can't spare the time, so I suppose he'll have to make his own way home. We were on our way to Rhodes to take part in a film, and Thor is anxious to get on.'

'Thor?' He had pronounced the name the Scandinavian way with a silent aitch.

'Thor Cameron. He's the skipper.'

Zara looked round the deck, thinking how marvellous it would be to sail over the deep blue waters of the Mediterranean in this beautiful boat. She said as much to Tony.

He grinned at her. 'It's a ship, not a boat.'

'So when does a boat become a ship?' she teased.

His mouth twisted into a comical look of dismay. 'Blowed if I know. How about going to the café in the harbour for a drink?'

'OK. Thanks.'

She went along with him as he walked tall beside her, wanting everyone to see that she was with him. Zara gave a hidden smile of amusement; it was a long time since she had been with anyone so young and unsophisticated, although he was probably only about her own age of twenty-two. I'm getting old, she thought.

At the café she drew Tony out to talk about himself, which he did happily enough, saying that he had been to university to study science but hadn't felt like going straight into a career so had taken this job for a few months. 'The pay is terrible,' he told her confidentially. 'But it's great being at sea, especially when we're under sail with no need to use the engines.'

'I can imagine.' She smiled at him. 'You'll have to be careful you don't get hooked, or all those years at university will be wasted.'

'I wouldn't mind,' he said a little wistfully. 'Thor has a really good life.'

'The captain? Does he own the boat—ship?'

Tony frowned. 'I shouldn't think so. The *Spirit* belongs to a company that has a whole fleet of sailing ships that it hires out for film and television work. And it does advertisements and promotional work; that kind of thing.'

They talked for a while longer, then Zara said, 'I'm afraid I'll have to go.'

'Are you working at the club tonight?'

She nodded and sighed. 'Yes, I'm afraid so.'

'Don't you like working there?'

'I hate it,' she admitted frankly.

'Why don't you leave, then?'

'I would if I could. Originally I had an act with another girl and we got a booking to appear in a club on a tourist complex in Sousse in Tunisia. But we hadn't been there very long when my friend's mother became ill and she had to fly back home. We only had enough money between us for the one fare, so I stayed on, but the club didn't want just me so they kicked me out. I was on the point of trying to hitchhike home when I heard about this job. Marcel—he's the singer—advanced me the train fare, and now that I've paid that back to him I'm saving up for my fare back to England.'

'Do you need much? I've got a few pounds——'

Zara quickly reached out and touched his hand. 'Thanks, Tony, that's very sweet of you, but I've almost got enough now.' She gave a rueful shrug. 'I shall have to leave soon anyway; there's an Arab who's started making a nuisance of himself. I don't think he's the type I can hold off for very long, so I shall go as soon as I can.'

'But you'll be at the club tonight?'

'Yes. It's pay-day.' She stood up and held out her hand. 'It was nice meeting you, Tony. And thanks for showing me over the ship. I envy you.'

Several members of the crew were in the club again that evening, including a tall man with red-gold hair and startling blue eyes, who Zara thought she hadn't seen before until she realised it was the man in uniform without his hat on. But Ali Messaad was also in the audience, sitting at the same table as before. The crew, though, were at the other side of the room and she had no excuse to go up to them, whereas the Arab was sitting right on the edge of the floor where she could hardly avoid him.

All the time she was dancing Zara was aware of his dark eyes watching her, and she had never felt so naked in her life. In the Cockney number, wearing a very short pearly-queen-type dress and a straw hat, she was supposed to go round the audience offering flowers to sell. She tried to avoid the Arab by dancing by him, but he reached out and caught her wrist in a vice-like grip, hurting her as he jerked her towards him. He murmured something she didn't understand, then pushed something down the front of her bodice and quite openly put his hand over her breast before he let her go. The men around him laughed as Zara pulled away, her face flaming, with anger as much as embarrassment. Pulling the object out of her dress, she flung it back in the man's grinning face without even looking at it. His expression immediately changed, becoming cold with rage.

Zara danced away, her heart thumping, knowing it had probably been the wrong thing to do. She should have taken whatever it was and played for time, instead of showing open contempt. But the disgusting man had openly humiliated her, so why shouldn't she do the same to him?

She went on with her part in the show but she saw that Messaad had left his seat and gone over to talk to the owner of the club, although it seemed to be more of an argument than a talk, with both men gesticulating excitedly. But then Zara saw the Arab and the men with him leave and she gave a sigh of relief. If the owner had stuck out against him then maybe things were going to be OK after all.

Feeling much happier, Zara performed her part in the show with far more enthusiasm and gave the crew members a cheerful wave as she ran off after the last show. But when she had changed and went to leave Zara found that her handbag had disappeared from the dressing-room. She searched everywhere but knew from the beginning that it was no use; the bag had been stolen. Her face pale, she told Marcel.

'Have any of the other girls' bags been taken?'

'No, it's just mine.'

An odd look came into his eyes, quickly hidden, and he shrugged. 'I'll tell the owner and I expect he'll tell the police, but I wouldn't hold out much hope of getting it back. Did you have much money in it?'

'No.' Zara shook her head slowly, her eyes fixed almost accusingly on his face. 'But I had my cheque-book and credit card in it. And my passport.'

'Well, you can always get replacements for those,' he said brusquely. 'If you're ready to leave, let's go.'

'What about our wages?'

Marcel's eyelids flickered. 'I didn't have time to go to the bank today. I'll pay you tomorrow.'

'The banks are closed tomorrow,' Zara pointed out, her voice hardening.

'So I'll pay you the day after. Are you coming or not?'

'I'll need some money to pay my hotel bill,' she told him. 'I can't give them a cheque now that my bag's been taken.'

'That's your problem,' he said impatiently, and not without a touch of malice. He turned away. 'I'm taking Danielle home now; either come with us or not.'

Zara had no choice but to go; she couldn't even afford a taxi now. As she walked grimly along she fumed with anger, knowing that this had been done deliberately at Ali Messaad's instigation. She thought of going to the police, but what good would that do if he was some local bigwig? They would put her down as a cheap foreigner making a fuss about nothing, and give her no protection. Was there a British consulate in Oran? Zara didn't know and didn't even have the money for a phone call to find out. And even if she went to them it would probably take days for her identity to be proved and a new passport supplied to her. And without the passport she couldn't draw any money from the bank.

Marcel left them at the door of the hotel, and as they went in the proprietor called them over and asked them to pay their bills, a thing he had never done at night before. Danielle paid hers and went up to the room, leaving Zara to explain about her stolen bag. The man frowned and looked unhappy, but said that if she couldn't pay she must leave.

Zara's head came up. 'All right, I'll go in the morning,' she said shortly.

'You must go now.'

She stared at him and he looked away, unable to meet her eyes. 'You cannot throw me out on to the street at night. I won't go!' Putting her hands on the desk, she leaned forward and said earnestly, 'Look, I know you've been forced into this. But you have daughters of your own; would you turn one of them out on the streets to face that man?'

He gave her a sheepish look and put his hands up to his face, pulling at the loose skin around his jawline. 'They will probably kill me—but all right, you can stay tonight. But first thing tomorrow you must go.'

Zara nodded, almost dizzy with relief. 'Yes, all right. Thank you.' She hesitated, then tried, 'Can I use your phone?'

But that was going too far. 'It isn't working.'

Managing to keep the contempt out of her eyes, she gave him a brief nod. There was still Danielle. Running up the stairs to their room, Zara stopped in astonishment when she saw that Danielle was hurriedly packing.

'What are you doing? Where are you going?'

'Leaving. I do not wish to share with you any longer. I go to stay with my friends.'

'But you can't just walk out on me,' Zara said, more in amazement than anger.

'I go if I wish,' Danielle stated stubbornly.

'Well, will you lend me some money so that I——?'

'No. I never get it back.'

'Then take me with you to stay with your friends,' Zara pleaded. 'Just for a couple of days until I can find somewhere else.'

'No, they would not want you.'

'But you can't just leave me to that man. I wouldn't walk out on you if you needed me.'

But no matter what she said Danielle wouldn't listen. She'd made up her mind that Zara was bad news and there was no way she was going to get involved. Within ten minutes she had packed all her belongings and gone.

Standing at the window, Zara watched her drive away in a taxi and wondered what on earth she was going to do. This Ali Messaad must be a powerful man if he could arrange all this since she'd thrown his gift back at him earlier. And an angry one, too. Zara shivered, suddenly terribly afraid. Even if she gave the man what he wanted it might not be the end of it. She had heard too many horrifying stories not to be aware that white slavery still went on. Girls would be drugged until they were hooked on it and then used as prostitutes. If that happened your life was as good as over; there was only total degradation left.

Her eyes went longingly across the harbour to where the *Spirit of the Wind* lay. There were Englishmen there, men who might protect her, if only she could reach them. And the boat would soon be leaving Oran. If she could get aboard it the captain might take her on as crew to the next port. Hope flared in Zara's heart. Confident that she had found her way out, she began to plan how she could get out of the hotel unseen and reach the ship.

Being very thin and very fit was a great help when climbing out of a tiny window at the back of the hotel. It was still dark, but dawn was on the horizon. The window was high off the ground but Zara hung from her fingertips and dropped the last couple of feet. She was dressed entirely in dark clothes: jeans and a long-sleeved sweater, her hair hidden beneath a dark head-scarf. Groping around in the dark, she found the bundle that she had dropped out first. There wasn't much inside it—just a few clothes and her dancing shoes. She hadn't dared to bring more.

She stayed very still until her eyes had become accustomed to the dark. Far down at the entrance to the alley she thought she saw a figure outlined against the dim light, which meant that that way was probably barred to her. But she had spent enough time in Oran looking out of the hotel window to know the layout of the

buildings all around. Keeping to the shadows, she crept
down the alley a short way, then into the yard of another
building, crossed it, and climbed over another wall into
an alley on the far side. A cat mewed suddenly and ran
from almost under her feet, frightening Zara to death.
She stood very still, pressed against the wall, afraid to
move until she was sure that no one had taken any notice.
Then she went on again, heading through the back alleys
towards the harbour. When she reached the main street,
which she had to go down, Zara stopped to take a
yashmak from her bundle and put it on. It was the double
veil worn by devout Moslem women, and which left only
the eyes uncovered. Zara had bought it as a souvenir
when she'd first come to North Africa and had had no
idea that she would ever need to actually wear it. It was
too short for her and she had to hunch up inside it
whenever she saw any one, but it was still very early and
there were few people about so she made quite good
progress, trying to curb the constant need to look over
her shoulder to see if she was being followed.

The dawn rose as she padded along in thonged sandals,
trying not to hurry too much, to look as natural as she
could. A car turned into the main street, going slowly
as if it was looking for someone. Panic-stricken, Zara
scuttled behind a pile of crates and hid until it had gone
by. Then she peeped out and saw it was a police car
going on its rounds. Her heart descended slowly towards
something like its rightful place and she went on her way
again.

She was pretty certain the ship wouldn't have left or
the crew would hardly have been in the nightclub last
night, but still felt a great sense of relief when it came
in sight. Her eyes searched the deck anxiously, wondering if there was anyone on watch, and whether he

would let her go aboard. Zara looked carefully around behind her before descending the steps from the harbour wall to the wharf, but there was no one in sight who looked at all dangerous. Going quickly down the steps, she ran to the ship and up the gangplank in a sudden last burst of fear that she might yet be stopped.

The panic carried her towards the companion-way leading below but she came to an abrupt halt as a voice called out, 'Stop!' in a tone that brought instant obedience.

Swinging round, she saw the tall man who she immediately, and rightly, guessed to be the captain, Thor Cameron. He came striding up to her and caught hold of her arm. 'What do you want here?'

He spoke in French and she realised that he thought her a native woman. 'I'm English. Oh, please you must help me. I'm in terr——'

'Who are you?' he snapped out.

'My name's Zara Beaumont. I came to ask you to take me with you wherever you're going. I've got to get away from Oran. There's a man who——'

'Come into the light.' He began to pull her towards the lantern at the head of the gangway but Zara hung back, still afraid of being recognised.

'Please; couldn't we go into a cabin?'

The captain hesitated, but then nodded. Still holding her arm, he led her down to the big main cabin and turned on the lights. 'Take off that thing,' he ordered.

Dropping her bundle on the floor, Zara did as he asked, revealing her slim figure. Then she undid the scarf and let her hair tumble down to her shoulders in a rich golden cascade.

'I thought so; you're the girl from the nightclub.'

'Yes, that's right. I——'

But he gave her no time to go on. His face hardening, Thor Cameron said, 'You needn't think you can come here looking for a free ride. We don't take passengers.'

'But I'd be happy to work my passage. Your cook's in hospital so I could do the cooking for you. I know how.'

He gave a harsh laugh, his lean, suntanned features derisive. 'I very much doubt that. And how did you know our cook was in hospital?'

'Tony told me. Please, I have to get away from here.'

'Not on this ship you don't,' he said in a tone that you didn't argue with. 'And keep away from my crew in future. Pick up your things and get ashore.'

'But you don't understand. There's a man, an Arab. He saw me in the nightclub and he won't take no for an answer. I *have* to get away from here.'

'So get on a plane or a train or a bus. There's plenty of ways out of Oran.'

'But I don't have any money and I——'

'And you thought you'd hitch an easy free ride with us. No way. This is an all-male ship and I don't want any females around upsetting the crew.'

'But I wouldn't. I'd do exactly what you told me and I'd get off at the first stop,' she pleaded.

But his face had set into implacable lines and he gave a snort of derision. 'There are women like you in every port in the world. The answer's still no. Get your things and go.' And when Zara made no move to do so he swept up the yashmak and her bundle and thrust them into her hands. Then he caught her wrist and began to pull her towards the door.

'No, please.' Zara hung back, close to tears.

'You heard me; you're not coming on this ship.'

Catching hold of the door-frame, Zara clung to it and screamed out, 'Tony! Tony, help!'

'Why, you little——' Thor Cameron jerked her forward and slung her over his shoulder.

But a tousled head had appeared in the passageway. 'You called me, Skipper?'

'No, I didn't. Go back to your cabin.'

'Tony, it's me. Don't let him put me ashore!' Zara yelled out. She tried to push herself off the captain's shoulder but was held in too strong a grip.

'Zara? What are you doing here?'

'You've got to help me. I'm in terrible trouble.'

'And *you'll* be in worse if you don't get back to your cabin,' the captain threatened Tony.

Pushing past him, he carried Zara up on deck. She beat at his back with her fists and struggled wildly. 'You can't do this. You're British. You've *got* to protect me. I don't have anyone else to go to for help.' But he crossed the deck, went down the gangway and dumped her unceremoniously on the wharf.

'Now get going.'

'You rotten swine!' Zara kicked him hard on the shins although he hardly felt it with her sandalled foot. 'Do you know what you're condemning me to?'

Tony came hurrying up to them. 'Skipper? What's happened?'

'Get her things,' he was ordered.

Puzzled, he did so, and Zara grabbed the yashmak from him and hastily put it on. It was almost light now and there were people about, some of them looking over at them curiously, and it was her only disguise, her only chance.

'I don't understand. What's going on?' Tony demanded.

'Get back on board.'

'But I——'

Thor Cameron turned to face him. 'I said get back on board. And keep away from this woman; she's just a cheap little trickster who'll tell any lie to get what she wants.' For a moment Tony hesitated, looking from Zara's pleading eyes to Thor Cameron's determined thrust of chin. Then he nodded—and went back on the ship. The captain turned to her. 'I don't know what your game is, but you're not going to play it on my ship. So just get lost. If you try to come on board again I'll call the police and have you thrown off.' And he turned his broad back on her and followed Tony back on the ship, standing guard at the gangway to make sure she kept away.

CHAPTER TWO

ZARA stood on the wharf, clutching her bundle and staring up at Thor Cameron's figure on the bridge of the ship, unable to believe that he had so brusquely rejected her pleas for help. Moving back to the harbour wall, she leant against it, feeling suddenly drained of strength. All through her nerve-racking escape from the hotel and her long, anxious walk through the town she had been so sure that she would find sanctuary on the ship. It had never even occurred to her that the captain might refuse her. Now what was she going to do?

Her first thought was to stay where she was in the hope that he might relent, but she almost immediately dismissed the idea; there was no way a man as determined as that was going to change his mind. Zara tried to think what was best to do. She was afraid to go back into the town to try and find out if there was a British agency that would help her. She didn't speak Arabic at all and her French was poor, so it meant going to the tourist information office to find someone who spoke English and Ali Messaad was sure to have someone watching the place. Well, OK, if she didn't have any money she at least had two feet; she could walk to the next town. And she had better get going while it was still early and she had the advantage of still being thought to be in the hotel.

Her mind made up, Zara bent to pick up her bundle, then grew still as she saw a flurry of movement at one of the portholes near the stern. Giving a quick glance up at the deck, she saw that the captain was still watching her, but then he turned away for a moment as someone came on deck to join him. It was Tony's face at the porthole. He waved and then held up a piece of paper with something scrawled on it in large letters: 'Go to the café.' As Zara nodded vigorously Tony gave her a thumbs-up sign and disappeared again. Her heart soared with hope, but Zara kept her shoulders bent, as if still in deep dejection, as she made her way slowly back up the steps to the harbour wall and along to the café.

It was open, of course; it was one of those places that never seemed to close. There were tables under sun-faded parasols outside and the rich smell of fresh coffee filling the morning air. It made Zara drool; she would have given a great deal for a cup, but she had no money so she had to find herself a quiet, hidden corner near by in the shade. Here she settled down to wait for Tony and just prayed that he wouldn't be long, and that he might have thought of some way to help her.

She had a long wait; it was almost three hours before Tony came into view and she had become sure that Thor Cameron had prevented him from coming. She was almost on the point of giving him up and leaving. The sun was high and hot and the smell from the rubbish bins near by was becoming difficult to take. Tony ambled nonchalantly into view, some letters in his hand, but once he had passed the corner of the café and was out of sight of the ship he stood still and looked sharply round at the customers.

'Tony. Over here,' Zara called.

'You haven't been waiting there all the time, have you?' he asked as Zara got stiffly to her feet. 'Why didn't you wait inside the café?'

'No money. Be an angel and buy me a Coke, would you, please? I'm so hot and thirsty.'

'Of course.' They went inside and Zara sat down at a table tucked away in a dark corner, facing the door so that she could see anyone who came in. 'I thought you said you had enough money,' Tony said as he came to join her after buying the drinks.

'I did, but my handbag was stolen from the club last night. It had my cheque-book and credit card in it, so I've no means of getting any cash.'

'Didn't you go to the police?'

'No, I wasn't able to.' And she told him the whole story.

'This Arab,' he interrupted at one point. 'Was he the man who pulled you on to his lap last night?' And, when Zara nodded, 'I saw you throw something back at him. I wondered what had happened. I don't suppose he liked that.'

'No, he didn't. And I'm certain it was him who arranged for my bag to be taken and for me to be thrown out of the hotel.'

'He did that, too?'

'Yes.' Zara described how she had sneaked out of the hotel. 'Luckily, I had the yashmak; if I hadn't I'm sure I would have been spotted almost straight away and someone would have reported back to Messaad. But I was able to get through the town and down to the harbour to your ship. I'm sorry if I got you into trouble but I didn't know where else to go. I suppose it was silly, but I'd convinced myself that I only had to ask and your captain would have let me sail with you. Because you're all British, you see.'

'Didn't you tell the skipper all this?'

'I tried to, but he wouldn't listen. I don't think he even believed me. He certainly didn't want to know.'

Tony stood up impetuously. 'I'll go back and talk to him. When I've explained all the details he'll *have* to let you come with us.'

Putting a restraining hand on his arm, Zara said, 'Thanks, Tony, but it wouldn't do any good. He'd just say that I'd spun you a whole web of lies.'

'Well, there must be some way I can help.' He sat down again, his brow creasing into a frown as he tried to think. 'How about if I came with you in a taxi to the airport and paid for your fare home? I could do it on my credit card, and you could pay me back when you get your money sorted out.'

Zara smiled at him, her faith in humanity partially restored. 'Thanks, Tony, I really appreciate that. But it wouldn't be any use either, I'm afraid. You see, my passport was also in my bag, so I can't get out of the country by any of the normal ways. And if this Ali Messaad is such a high official and has as much power as he seems to have, then I'm sure he'll be on the watch for me at the airport and the station. And he could easily accuse me of some trumped-up charge, have me arrested and put under his jurisdiction.'

They were both gloomily silent for a moment, until Tony said, 'The ship seems to be your only hope, then.'

'No, I'd already decided to walk to the next town, and then——'

'You can't do that,' Tony interrupted sharply. 'It's miles. And you'd stand out like a sore thumb, even with that thing on.'

'But if you could lend me some money I could perhaps get a bus to Algiers. There'd be a British embassy there where I could go for help.'

'Can you speak French or Arabic?' Tony demanded.

'No, but I'm sure I could manage to get by.'

He shook his head impatiently. 'Wait a minute; let me think,' he ordered.

Zara sat in silent obedience, beginning to feel tired from her sleepless night, her tummy reminding her that it had been a long time since she'd eaten. But they were the least of her worries.

After several minutes of frowning concentration, Tony leaned across the table towards her and spoke in a determined whisper. 'I shall just have to smuggle you on board,' he announced.

Zara's eyes opened like an owl's and her mouth dropped open behind the concealing black veil. 'Can you do that?'

'Yes, I know a way.'

'But the captain?'

'We'll be leaving on the night's tide and he has to go up to the harbour-master's office to clear Customs before we sail. I can get you on board then.'

Zara stared into his face, her eyes suddenly blazing with hope. 'Are you sure? What if one of the other men in the crew sees me?'

Tony thought again. 'You're wearing jeans under that veil thing, aren't you? If you wear a thick sweater and put your hair up under some kind of hat they might think you're one of us. And we're waiting for some last-minute stores so you'll probably be able to slip aboard among the loaders.'

'Tony, you're a genius,' Zara said in heartfelt admiration, her eyes blazing with excitement.

Tony grinned, catching her mood, his own eyes lighting. 'I think we can do it. Now let's see——'

But Zara's face had fallen. 'No, it's no good. It's marvellous of you to suggest it, Tony, but I can't possibly let you do it. You'd get into terrible trouble with Thor Cameron. He might even make you leave the ship when he finds out.'

Squaring his shoulders manfully, Tony said, 'Well, that's a chance I'll have to take. And at least I'd be with you when he threw us off. And we'd be in a different port. I'm willing to risk it if you are.'

'Yes, of course, but *I've* got nothing to lose. Are you quite sure?'

'Absolutely.'

Her eyes lit at his positiveness and she gave him a dazzling smile that he couldn't see. 'OK, let's go for it. But you've got to promise that if and when I'm found you're to say that you know nothing about it,' she warned. 'There's no point in you getting into trouble unnecessarily.'

They discussed their plans further, getting it down to as much detail as they could. There were some shops near by where Tony bought a big, loose sweater and a peaked sailor's cap which Zara put in her bundle, but then he had to hurry back to the ship, afraid that the captain might suspect him of meeting her. He gave her some money and, after he'd gone, Zara used it to buy something to eat and then posted his letters, afterwards finding a ladies' loo without an attendant and spending the rest of the day inside its very smelly confines. It was almost dark when she came out at last, and Zara took in great lungfuls of fresh air, vowing that she'd never go in a place like that again as long as she lived if she could possibly avoid it.

Still afraid that Ali Messaad might find her, Zara hurried to the café near the harbour and in the sheltered

spot where she'd waited that morning changed the
yashmak for the sweater and cap. Making sure that her
hair was completely tucked out of sight, she smeared
some dirt on her face and hands to hide their whiteness
and then, heart thumping, walked along in the shadow
of the wall to the steps leading down to the wharf. There
were several men on the deck of the ship, Tony and the
captain among them, but there was no sign of the lorry
with the stores. Terribly afraid that it might have been
and gone, Zara sat down to wait, desperate thoughts of
swimming after the boat and pulling herself aboard if
it sailed away running through her mind.

There was the sound of a rough-engined vehicle, and
a big covered lorry came trundling slowly along the
wharf. It pulled up alongside the ship and the captain
immediately snapped out an order, telling the men to
get the stuff on board as quickly as possible. He watched
the work begin, then pulled on a jacket and ran down
the gangway, but instead of going to the harbour-master's
office by walking along the wharf he came straight
towards the steps where Zara was hiding.

Hastily she fled back behind the wall and scuttled
several yards along towards the sea, bent double to avoid
being seen. She could hear Thor Cameron's feet running
briskly up the stone steps and could do nothing but cower
down, hoping he wouldn't see her. For a heart-stopping
moment he seemed to hesitate at the top of the steps,
but then he turned in the opposite direction and strode
briskly away.

For a few moments Zara stayed where she was, feeling
almost sick with relief, but then remembered that the
hardest part of all, getting aboard the ship, still had to
be accomplished.

In the event, it was easy. Keeping to the shadowy side of the steps, she ran down to the lorry, waited until there was no one there, then swung a box of what smelt like oranges on her shoulder and carried it up the gangway, her arm covering her face. Tony was where he said he would be, at the head of the companion-way, and he quickly took her down to the tiny cabin behind the galley where the cook normally slept. Leaving her there, he went back to his post, his momentary absence unnoticed.

The cabin was on the starboard side of the ship, away from the wharf, but Zara didn't dare to put on a light and had to grope to get under the bunk, curling herself into as small a ball as possible and pulling her bundle of belongings in behind her.

It was very dark and damp, so she was glad of the sweater, and the slight movement of the ship felt strange. The noises from the deck came through to the cabin and eventually she heard the lorry drive away. She waited tensely, willing the ship to get under way. Suddenly the door was flung open and a man stood in the doorway, framed by the light in the passageway. It wasn't the captain; this man had hairy bare legs and large feet in a pair of old trainers. It must be the first mate, the man she'd seen sunning himself with Tony the first time she'd come on board. Resisting a panicky need to try and make herself even smaller, Zara lay very still. But he must have only given the cabin a cursory glance before he shut the door again and went on with his inspection.

Shortly afterwards the engine started and they were under way.

The engine ran for only about half an hour, then the sails went up and the only sounds were the creaking of wood and the slap of waves against the side as the ship came into its own and bowed to the wind. The floor seemed to move a great deal, but luckily Zara's stomach stayed where it was supposed to. Perhaps she was a good sailor; she'd never had the opportunity to find out before. The extreme tension gone, she even managed to sleep for a few hours until woken by cramp and thirst.

Tony had told her she must stay hidden for at least twelve hours, until it would be too late for them to turn back to Oran. But Zara had privately determined to stay in concealment until they reached the next port and then slip ashore, so that Tony wouldn't get into trouble. She didn't think she'd been asleep all that long—it was still dark outside, but she was unable to see her watch. Unable to bear the discomfort any longer, she wriggled out from under the bunk and crept into the empty galley where she stole a can of Coke before hurrying back to her hiding-place. Feeling safer, she lay down on the bunk to sleep again and it was broad daylight when she woke for the second time.

She had a more pressing need now and Tony hadn't thought to provide her with a receptacle. Crossing her legs tightly, Zara listened to the sounds of someone cooking in the galley and drooled over the aromas. But presently the appetising smells changed to those of burning, followed by a great deal of swearing. Whoever was doing the cooking sounded as if he was getting into a terrible state. The crew seemed to think so too by the grumbles and complaints that later came through the wall when they all came down to eat.

Zara just *had* to use the loo. When all was quiet again she opened the door and peeped out. The galley was empty. She crept through it towards where the showers and loos—'heads', Tony had called them when he'd showed her round—were situated in the forward part of the ship, not far from the galley. Luckily she didn't have to pass any of the other cabins to reach them, and got there safely. The heads were right next to the showers; when Zara came out she looked at the showers longingly, she felt so hot and dirty. What the hell, she thought, and dived in the nearest, throwing her clothes outside on the floor. The water was ice-cold, making her gasp at first, but it felt like heaven on her parched, dusty skin. Finding a piece of soap, Zara lathered herself all over, then closed her eyes as she tilted back her head to let the water cascade over her, rinsing away the soap.

'Didn't you hear me say no showers during the day? I don't give orders for fun. I——' The rings rattled as the shower curtain was jerked back, and Zara found herself staring into the captain's startled face. But then his eyes left her face and swept down the length of her body.

Grabbing the curtain from his slack hold, Zara pulled it across herself, hiding as much as possible behind it.

'Get out of here!' she yelled at him.

'What the hell are you doing here?' he thundered at the same time.

For a moment they glared at each other, but it was the captain who spoke first. 'I might have known. Get out of there and get dressed.'

'Not with you standing there, I'm not.'

He gave a derisive snort. 'It's a bit damn late to start being prudish.' But he moved away and went into the galley.

Turning off the shower, Zara stood in trepidation for a few moments, just praying that he wouldn't turn the ship round and take her back to Oran.

'Hurry up in there,' he called curtly.

'All right, I'm coming.' She looked round. 'Er—Mr Cameron—Skipper, do you happen to have a towel handy?'

There was a short, sharp imprecation, but after a moment he came and handed her a towel. 'Now hurry it up,' he ordered through gritted teeth.

When a man spoke like that you hurried. Within five minutes Zara was dried, dressed, and had come hesitantly into the saloon. The ceiling was made of glass panels through which the sun shone in a great beam. It lay across the captain where he stood, tall and very blond, his body in just a T-shirt and shorts, lean and tanned. That, and his short, fair beard, for a brief moment reminded Zara of a Viking raider of old, and she felt a *frisson* of fear, especially when she saw the anger in his ice-cold blue eyes. Trying to break the image, Zara gave him a tentative smile and said, 'Hi.'

It didn't work. If anything, his scowl deepened as he said, 'Do you know the punishment for stowing away on a ship?'

'I didn't want to stow away; it was your fault—you forced me to it.'

His eyes opened wide in astonishment. '*I* forced you to——?'

'Yes, because if you'd listened to me and taken me on as crew then I wouldn't have had to sneak on board and hide,' Zara retorted spiritedly.

'Of all the barefaced cheek, you take the prize.' His face hardened. 'I suppose Tony smuggled you on board last night while my back was turned. I'm going to have something to say to that boy.'

'You're quite wrong,' Zara cut in. 'Tony didn't help me. I got on board by myself when the stores were being loaded.'

Thor gave a disbelieving laugh. 'You expect me to believe that?'

'It's true,' Zara protested, crossing her fingers behind
her back. 'I didn't need any help; it was easy.'

'And just where did you hide when you came on
board?'

He was watching her narrowly and Zara knew she had
to be careful; she didn't want to get Tony into trouble
if she could possibly avoid it. 'In the cook's cabin,' she
admitted. 'Tony told me that your cook had been taken
ill so I thought that would be a good place to hide.'

'I see. And you just happened to know where it was
by instinct, did you?'

'No,' she answered levelly. 'I've been on the ship
before. Tony gave me a tour round one day. He said that
interested visitors are often taken over the ship. There
was someone else with him that day; I think Tony said
he was the first mate. You can ask him if you don't believe me.'

'Strangely enough, I don't. How did you know when
the stores were coming aboard unless Tony told you?'
he demanded, suddenly firing the question at her.

'I'd been up on the harbour all day looking for an
opportunity,' Zara answered at once, keeping as near to
the truth as possible. 'When it got dark I waited by the
harbour steps. You almost trod on me when you came
ashore,' she couldn't resist adding derisively. 'As soon
as you were out of the way I just picked up a crate from
the lorry and carried it on the boat.'

'Ship,' he corrected automatically.

'Sorry, ship.'

'So it seems I'll have to have that talk with the first
mate instead of Tony.'

Zara blinked, not wanting to have anyone punished on her account. 'He didn't see me.'

'I hope he didn't.' Thor leaned towards her, suddenly full of menace. 'Because if I find that he or anyone else helped you, or even turned a blind eye to your coming aboard, then that man is off this ship at the next port. Which is where you're also getting off. Do I make myself clear?'

She nodded, full of heartfelt relief that he wasn't going to turn back to Oran. 'Yes. Thank you.'

Perhaps he read her mind, because he said, 'If it wasn't that I've already lost four days because of the cook's illness I'd take great pleasure in turning around and handing you over to the authorities in Oran. I don't know what sort of trouble you've got yourself into there, but I dislike having my ship used as a bolt-hole for common criminals.'

'I'm not a criminal,' Zara protested.

'What do you call yourself, then—a common hooker?' And his eyes swept disparagingly over her as she stood in jeans and sun-top, the material clinging to her where she wasn't quite dry.

Her face flamed. 'How dare you call me that? You have no right to insult me. I'm not——'

Stepping forward, he loomed over her. 'On this ship I do and say what I damn well like, and don't you forget it. And I still think that you seduced Tony into helping you to get aboard.'

'I didn't seduce him,' Zara denied hotly, her grey eyes flashing fire. 'And he didn't help me. No one did. The only person I asked for help was *you*—and you wouldn't give it to me when I so desperately needed it.'

They said the best method of defence was attack, and it seemed to work, because after studying her angry face for a moment Thor stepped back and put up a hand to his jaw, running it over his short beard. 'All right, now I have to decide what to do with you. I know what I'd like to do with you, but unfortunately ships aren't fitted with irons nowadays. What did you say your name is?'

'Zara. Zara Beaumont.'

He gave a small snort of disgust, evidently taking exception even to her name. 'You'd better go on using the cook's cabin,' he said brusquely. 'And make sure you stay there, away from my crew—especially Tony.'

'Yes. I——' She was about to offer to help with the cooking again, but thought she'd better not. 'Yes, OK.'

'Give me your passport.'

'I don't have it. I told you; it——'

'You don't what?' Thor's jaw thrust forward and he glared at her disbelievingly.

'It was stolen, along with my handbag. And all my money and my credit card were in there, too—that's why I couldn't just catch a plane in the normal way. I did tell you when I was on board yesterday morning, but I don't suppose you bothered to listen,' she finished bitterly.

'Where are your things?'

'What? In the cabin. But I——' She broke off as Thor swung away from her and strode down the corridor to throw open the door of the tiny cabin. Grabbing up her bundle, he pulled it open and dropped all the contents on to the bed, then began to search through them. 'Hey!' Zara protested as one of her gold dancing shoes was tossed aside in disgust. 'Watch it, will you? That's all I've got left in the world.'

But she might as well not have bothered as he went through the rest of her things and then searched the cabin to make sure she hadn't hidden anything away. Then

Thor turned on her, his face grim. 'Do you realise that without a passport you could be classed as a stateless person? And stateless people are never allowed to go on shore. I could be stuck with you on this ship for *years* before it's sorted out.'

Zara's face paled, but her chin came up as she said, 'Well, you don't have to look so unhappy about it; the thought of being on the same ship as you for any longer than necessary doesn't exactly grab me either. As soon as we reach a port where I can prove my identity and get another passport, then I'll be pleased to leave.'

'But in the meantime I'm stuck with you.'

'Yes.' She gave a sudden grin of pure relief. 'I'm afraid you are.'

Thor shot her a malevolent look and turned to leave, but as he reached the door leading from the galley Zara said, 'Please; where are we going?'

He paused. 'Not to England, if that's what you're hoping. But Tony would already have told you that. We're going to Rhodes.'

'Yes, he told me that, too. But where is your first stop on the way?'

'There are no "stops", as you call them. We've lost too much time already and we're heading straight there without any other ports of call.' And he turned to duck his head and go through the door.

To go and find Tony and interrogate him, Zara guessed, and only hoped that Tony would keep his head and lie convincingly. Well, there was nothing she could do about it now, either way. Feeling hungry, she made herself a sandwich and a big mug of coffee. Up on deck she heard someone shout out an order, and then the captain's voice. Telling the crew about her, presumably.

Tony hadn't been sent down below in disgrace so maybe he had managed to bluff it out. She certainly hoped so.

After she'd finished eating Zara set to and cleaned up the galley, which was in a terrible mess with pans not properly washed and the working surfaces still dirty. When the place was spotlessly clean she went to the foot of the companion-way, then hesitated, wondering if it would be all right to go on deck. Thor had told her to stay in the cabin, but he surely couldn't mean her to stay below for the whole voyage. And anyway, she'd been cooped up in that cabin long enough. Deciding that, if she was going to break any rules, she'd better break them at the start, Zara ran lightly up the companion-way and out on to the deck.

The late-afternoon sun, rich and red, slanted across the ship, colouring the taut sails deep gold, catching the foaming crests of the bow waves and turning the flying spray into a million sparkling diamonds. The wind was fresh and clean, blowing her hair about her head like Medusa tendrils. It was a world away from the heat and smells of Oran, a whole way of life away from the nightclub and the threat of Ali Messaad. Zara took in a long, deep breath and knew that there was nowhere else she would rather be at this moment. Silly tears of thankfulness came to her eyes but she brushed them quickly away and looked around her.

Tony had told her that there were only seven men in the crew, and all of them, except the captain, seemed to be on deck. They had been talking and laughing but stopped abruptly when she appeared. Most of them, Zara realised, she had already seen at the nightclub. Going up to the ginger-haired first mate she stuck out her hand. 'Hello. I'm Zara Beaumont. I hope I didn't get you into any trouble by sneaking on board.'

He hesitated for a moment, then gave a rueful grin and shook her hand. 'I've had worse bawling outs. I'm James Mackenzie but they all call me Mack,' he told her in a Scots accent that underlined his name. He didn't exactly say 'welcome aboard', but there was no anger in his eyes and this was explained when he added, 'Tony has told us your story. Come on, I'll introduce you to these other sea-dogs.'

There was the engineer, Ken, and the second mate, a young man from Sweden called Arne Huss, both of whom greeted her with broad grins. As did Tony and the other two deck-hands, Steve Johnson from England and Pete Keats from Australia. Thor, Mack, Ken, Arne, Steve, Pete and Tony. As Zara recited the names to stick them in her mind she felt rather like Snow White meeting the seven dwarfs. Not that any of these men could be classed as even short; they were all quite tall and well-muscled, which was easy to see as none of them wore more than a pair of shorts. Maybe they didn't even wear that much when they were at sea and had put on the shorts for her benefit. Another similarity was that they all had beards or were growing them. The men had been crowding round her, but Mack said warningly, 'The skipper,' and they suddenly became busy with various tasks again.

Thor had come up the companion-way from his cabin and walked down the deck towards her. Among these men, he was still very tall; among dwarfs, he would have been a giant.

'I thought I told you to keep out of the way,' he said shortly.

Zara's chin came up. 'I needed some fresh air. You can't expect me to stay below the whole time, surely?'

But she spoke reasonably and kept her voice lowered, not wanting to provoke him.

But he frowned and said, 'I've been working out a timetable when it will be convenient for you to use the showers and take exercise. Come to my cabin and I'll give it to you.'

Meekly she followed him along the deck to the narrow companion-way leading to his cabin. Thor didn't even bother to go down the steps, just put a hand on the rope, his feet on either side, and slid down. Not having his expertise or even her sea-legs yet, Zara rather awkwardly turned round and went down the steps backwards. His cabin was very compact, very neat, with the one bunk carefully made and no clothes lying around. Against the forward bulkhead was a big chart table and the ship's radio desk, with beside it a curtained alcove screening the captain's private shower-room. There was also a writing-table with shelves of books above it and, alongside his bunk, a seating area with a table. The latter in case he wanted to eat alone, Zara guessed, and wondered whether Thor ate with the crew or held himself aloof from them. They certainly seemed to hold him in some awe, but whether it was respectful or not she didn't yet know.

There was a pad of paper on his desk. Going over to it, Thor tore off the top sheet and handed it to her. 'You'll keep to these times.'

Zara glanced through it and frowned. 'Only one shower a day—in this heat?'

'Water is the most precious commodity aboard a ship. The crew take only one shower a day and so will you,' he replied curtly.

'OK, fair enough.' She read on and saw, underlined, that she was not to leave her cabin during the two night-watches. 'What's a nightwatch?' she asked, puzzled.

'Time on board a ship is divided into watches, each of four hours long,' Thor explained. 'A watch is a collective name for the men who are actually running the ship at that time while the others eat and sleep. On this ship the watches are four hours on and four hours off.'

'So everyone works a twelve-hour day.'

He nodded. 'Yes, that's right.'

'How about you?' she asked curiously.

'I'm always on watch,' he informed her, his eyes narrowing. 'So don't think you can sneak into one of the crew's cabins while my back's turned.'

Her fingers tightened on the sheet of paper as Zara fought to control a spurt of sudden anger. 'Look, you have entirely the wrong idea about me,' she said forcefully. 'If I were a—a hooker I wouldn't have had to run away from Oran. I would have given the Arab what he wanted and that would have been the end of it. It was because I wouldn't come across that he got nasty and created all these problems to try to force me to give in to him.'

Thor gave her a sceptical look, in no way convinced. 'Are you saying that you're an innocent?' he asked in a tone of frank disbelief.

She flushed. 'I'm saying that I don't sell myself.'

His lip curled sardonically. 'But you're not above seducing Tony into helping you to stow away on this ship.'

'I did not seduce him—and he didn't help me.'

His eyes, of a deep blue, as blue as the sea, regarded her steadily for a long moment. Zara tried to meet them but blinked and looked down.

He gave a short laugh, his belief confirmed. 'I shall expect you to work to earn your passage,' he said grimly.

'I've already offered to do that.'

Ignoring her, he went on, 'As you'll see on that list, you are to clean out the crew's heads and showers every morning after they've used them and while they're having breakfast. Then, when they've eaten, you can have your breakfast and afterwards clean out the galley. The same goes for lunch and the evening meal. And you can exercise on deck for one hour in the morning and again in the afternoon.'

Zara looked at the list interestedly. He had completely wasted his time in writing it, of course, because she had no intention of keeping to it. She would do the work very willingly, but there was no way she was going to stay cooped up down below, especially now she had had a brief experience of that wonderful breeze in her hair. Cheekily she said, 'Aye, aye, Cap'n,' and saluted.

But that was a mistake because Thor's eyes narrowed and he said menacingly, 'Just watch it, because I can make life on this ship even more unpleasant for you than it was in Oran.'

Zara very much doubted that but said meekly, 'Sorry. What am I supposed to call you, then?'

For a moment he hesitated, then said shortly, 'Skipper will do.' Turning to the desk, he picked up the notepad and a pen and held them out to her, saying, 'I want you to write down all the information that would have appeared on your passport. Your personal details—height and so on; the name and address of your next of kin, and, if you can remember, where and when your passport was issued.'

'All right.' She took the things from him, her hands brushing his.

His voice sharpened. 'You can give it to me tomorrow after breakfast and I'll radio through the details to the British consulate in Rhodes and ask them to issue a replacement.'

'Thank you.'

It was awkward carrying the things up the companion-way when the ship was moving, especially when she knew Thor was watching her, and Zara didn't make a very graceful job of it. Deciding that if this was her hour of exercise then she still had a lot of it due to her, she went and sat on a box in the bow, letting the breeze lift her hair and the strong smell of the sea fill her nostrils. Thor had followed her on deck, so the crew kept their distance, and she went to her cabin while they were having their meal. She would stick to his rules today and start breaking them tomorrow, Zara decided. She would have liked to talk to Tony, though, and presumably he felt the same because he slipped a note under her door:

I stuck to our story and said I hadn't helped you. He was angry but hasn't said that I'm fired. I think we've pulled it off. Tony.

Which they wouldn't have done if Thor had seen him putting the note under the door and had insisted on reading it, Zara thought wryly. Tearing the sheet of paper into minute pieces, she flushed it down the heads after Steve banged on her door and told her they'd finished eating. The galley was in the usual terrible mess and Ken, who had been detailed into taking over the cooking, hadn't even bothered to wash up. Well, at least there was one person who was really pleased she was on board, Zara thought with a grin as she cleared the place up before making herself an omelette.

She would have liked to go on deck to see the stars but instead took a magazine from the pile in the galley into her cabin and settled down to read. During the evening she heard some of the crew go into the galley for a nightcap, but presently all grew quiet. Zara lay awake, not at all tired, thinking that the girls would only just be starting the second show back in the nightclub. She felt no nostalgia for it. Suddenly the show-business world, one that she'd been pushed into by an ambitious mother and the only one she knew, seemed very brash and trivial. The glamour had rubbed off years ago but she had stuck it because there was nothing else, and there was always the receding hope that she would one day make it big, get in a West End show or something. Now she decided that when she got back to England she would try and do something else. Heaven only knew what it would be, but she would try.

She was so lost in her thoughts that she hardly heard the door opening, and it was only when the light from the passage showed that she turned over to look. 'Tony! What are you doing here? This is crazy.'

'Did you get my note?'

'Yes, but it was dumb to send it. Go back to your cabin.'

'I thought you'd want to talk.' He sounded injured, his voice unsteady. 'What did you tell Thor?'

She sat up. 'What we said. But I don't think he believes me. He may try to trip you up so you'd better watch it. And you'd better go back to your cabin for a start.' She couldn't see his face in the darkness but felt that there was an air of excitement about him and wondered if some of the others had put him up to this. 'Go on, go away.'

But instead he felt his way to the bunk and tried to put his arms round her. He'd been drinking whisky to give himself Dutch courage. 'I just wanted to give you a kiss goodnight,' he mumbled, trying to find her mouth.

She tried to push him away but he wouldn't go. Exasperated, Zara said, 'All right, just one kiss for helping me but then you've got to promise to go, OK?'

'OK.'

She tried to make it just a peck but Tony put his arms round her to give it the passionate works as he bent her back against the pillow. In danger of being asphyxiated, Zara tried to push him away, and could only be thankful as he suddenly jerked back. She took a couple of deep breaths and sat up again, but then the light snapped on and she found that the captain had pulled Tony away by his collar and was glaring at her out of furious blue eyes. He didn't say anything—he didn't have to: his eyes said it all. Then he pulled Tony out of the cabin, slammed the door and locked it from the outside.

'Oh, hell!' Zara gave an angry groan of frustration and buried her face in her hands.

CHAPTER THREE

THOR didn't let Zara out until the following morning. She had woken and dressed long ago. She had heard the crew gather to have their breakfast, their voices far more subdued than usual, and had expected him to unlock the door then, but he hadn't done so. She had waited, growing more nervous by the minute, but angry with herself for being afraid. After all, he couldn't eat her, could he? And he had said himself that there were no irons on the ship he could clap her into. But Thor had been furiously angry last night. Zara remembered the rage in his eyes and shivered, despite herself. When footsteps approached the cabin and the key turned in the lock at last she was sitting on the bunk, her elbows resting on her knees, her eyes fixed on the door.

When Thor pulled it open his face was cold and set. 'My cabin in ten minutes,' he ordered curtly, then strode away.

Zara washed in double-quick time and was waiting outside the captain's door with a minute to spare. So was Tony. He looked terrible, his face pale and haggard, dark circles round his eyes, and he leant against the wall as if his legs wouldn't hold him. His hair and his clothes were wet, as if someone had thrown a bucket of water over him. It didn't take much brain-work to guess who.

'What happened?' he said dazedly. 'I can hardly remember.'

'You were drunk,' Zara said unsympathetically. 'You must remember drinking last night.'

'I only had a couple of beers,' Tony protested.

'Plus the whisky,' she said drily.

He gave her a bewildered look. 'But I didn't——'

His words were cut off as the captain's door opened and he waved them inside, watching in silence as they came and stood in front of his desk. Like naughty schoolchildren, Zara thought with the resentment of innocence.

Thor walked round the desk but didn't sit down. He was so tall that his head almost brushed the ceiling. His contemptuous eyes went first to Zara and then to Tony. Zara lifted her chin defiantly but Tony blinked and looked sheepish. Thor didn't bother to ask for any explanations. 'You obviously both lied to me.' His eyes, scathingly cold, went to Zara. 'You couldn't have got aboard without help and it was Tony who gave it to you, as I suspected. You'll both be put off this ship as soon as we get to Rhodes.'

'But that isn't fair,' Zara protested. 'Tony was——'

Thor shot her a look that froze her words. 'I don't give a damn who's to blame or who seduced whom; I don't want either of you on my ship. I'm not having the *Spirit* fouled by dirt like you.'

The words were so insulting that Zara could only stare at him in open-mouthed astonishment.

'In the meantime you'll both be confined to——'

Anger shot through her in a tidal wave and Zara stepped forward, her eyes flashing furiously in her pale face. 'Now just you wait a minute! Who the hell do you think you are, passing judgement on us? Being the captain of this tin-pot little sailing boat doesn't make you God Almighty, even if you think it does.'

'Zara!' Tony caught hold of her arm to try and stop her, his voice anguished.

It was Thor's turn to stare in amazement. Probably no one had spoken to him like that in years. But it was the insult to his precious ship that got to him most. Leaning forward, he put his hands on the desk and glared at her furiously. 'This ship is one of the finest under sail in the world. But trust a little guttersnipe like you not to recognise beauty when you see it.'

Swept forward on a roller-coaster of indignation, Zara shot back, 'And trust a jumped-up deckswabber like you not to recognise the truth when you hear it.'

'Zara!' Tony gave a moan and tried to pull her away but she shook him off impatiently.

'Jumped-up deckswabber! Why, you little——' Thor began to stride round his desk towards her but a loud knock sounded on the door and Mack, the first mate, came in. 'What the hell do you want?' Thor demanded violently.

'Sorry, Skipper, but there's something I think you ought to know.'

'Later.'

Bravely disobeying the peremptory order, Mack said, 'But it concerns Tony. I found out his beer was laced with whisky last night.'

Thor turned to give him his attention, his brows drawn into a grim frown. 'Are you sure of this?'

'Yes. I knew it wasn't like Tony to drink so I made some enquiries.'

'Who did it?'

'Rather not say, Skipper. It was meant as a joke.'

'Oh, wouldn't you?' Thor's glare deepened and Zara thought for a minute that he wouldn't believe Mack, but he evidently trusted him because he said, 'All right. Come to my cabin again in half an hour.'

'Aye, aye, Skipper.' The mate turned and left, carefully not looking at either Tony or Zara.

When he'd gone, Thor turned his back on them and looked out of the window for a moment. He had a proper square window, not just a porthole as they had in the crew's cabins. Zara watched him with little hope; he had been so angry that she couldn't see the mate's intervention making the slightest difference. But when he faced them the furious rage had gone, although his eyes were still coldly angry. Addressing Tony, he said, 'It seems that you have been doubly a victim: of this girl's wiles and your shipmates' crass idea of humour. But you still lied to me about helping her to stow away, so whether or not I put you ashore at Rhodes will depend entirely on your behaviour for the rest of the voyage. And until we get there you'll be given all the worst jobs aboard ship to do. Have you anything to say about that?'

'No.' Tony gave a heartfelt sigh of relief. 'I'm sorry, Skipper. You won't have reason to complain again.'

'I'd better not. All right, you can go.'

Tony hesitated, looking from Thor to Zara. 'Skipper. It wasn't Zara's fault either. She was——'

'I said you can go.' Thor's voice would have frozen oil.

'Aye, aye, Skipper.' Tony turned and fled.

Going behind his desk again, Thor faced Zara, who instinctively squared her shoulders ready for the onslaught.

She wasn't mistaken. His bearded jaw thrust forward, Thor said forcefully, 'I knew you'd be trouble from the first moment I set eyes on you. That's why I refused to have you aboard my ship in the first place. And I was right; you've only been on board two days and you've already disrupted the whole crew.'

'It wasn't my fault. I——'

'Of course it was your fault!' he bawled at her, making her jump. 'You're a woman, aren't you? You're attractive, aren't you? It doesn't take more than that, especially with someone as young and green as Tony, so it's no good trying to put the blame on him.'

He glared at her, daring her to speak, but Zara had nothing to say. Part of what he said was true; she *had* been willing to use Tony in her desperate need to get away from Oran. So she stood silently facing him, but there was pride in every inch of her tall, slim figure.

'You will keep to the times and the list of duties I gave you,' he told her. 'But in future you will be locked in your cabin every night.'

Zara gave a small gasp. 'You can't do that. What if I'm taken ill or something?'

'Tough.'

She stared at him. 'And what if the ship sinks?'

His mouth twisted with sardonic amusement at such an impossibility. 'Then I'll guarantee to rescue you along with the ship's cat,' he said derisively. 'Now get out of here—and just remember that if you step out of line just once then you'll be locked in your cabin for the whole voyage. And don't think I can't do it,' he added as Zara began to open her mouth, 'because I can do any damn thing I like aboard this ship—and locking you up out of harm's way would give me great pleasure.'

Recognising an indomitable will when she met one, Zara gave up trying to reason with him and left the cabin.

Tony was waiting for her in the galley, his face anxious. 'What did he say?'

Zara pulled a face. 'What do you think? I'm to be locked in my cabin every night so that all you randy sailors can't get at me. I'll feel like an animal in a cage.'

Tony flushed. 'I'm sorry about that, Zara. If they hadn't made me drunk I wouldn't have—well, you know.'

'You wouldn't have dared,' she finished for him, and then felt sorry at the hurt look that came into his eyes. 'Oh, Tony, don't worry about it. It wasn't your fault. I expect they all thought it would be a huge joke to get you drunk and then egg you on. But at least they owned up, so it gives you another chance. Unless the captain changes his mind, of course,' she said gloomily.

'He won't,' Tony said positively. 'The skipper is always fair.'

'Well, at least he didn't cast us adrift in an open boat,' Zara agreed.

'I thought he'd personally throw you overboard when you called him a deckswabber,' Tony said in some awe. 'If one of the men had called him that he would probably have got his head knocked off.' He sat down on a bench and put his hands up to his own head. 'Lord, I feel terrible.'

'Hangover?'

He nodded dolefully. 'My head feels as if the ship's fog-horn is going off inside it.'

Zara smiled. 'Have you had any breakfast?'

Tony shuddered. 'No. I couldn't eat anything.'

'Nonsense,' she said briskly. 'You'll feel much better after you've eaten; I guarantee it.'

She made cheese omelettes with wholemeal bread freshly baked in the oven, and when she set the plates on the table Tony picked up his fork, suddenly finding his appetite. Zara went to sit on the bench opposite, but just then Mack walked into the galley.

'Any coffee going?'

'I'll make you some,' Zara offered.

'Thanks for coming to our rescue,' Tony said fervently. 'The skipper was going to send me home at Rhodes.'

The mate nodded and looked at their plates. 'That looks good.'

'Why don't you have mine?' Zara said diplomatically. 'I can easily make another omelette.'

She didn't have to make the offer twice. Mack sat down and tucked hungrily into the food, afterwards wiping the plate with a piece of bread. 'That's the best food I've tasted since we arrived in Oran. All the rest of the crew are hopeless as cooks and Ken seems to be the worst.' He raised an eyebrow at her. 'You wouldn't like to take on the job, would you?'

'I offered to,' Zara told him as she sat down to eat a fresh omelette. 'But the skipper said no. I wouldn't want to disobey him.'

'No, we don't want that.' Mack put a hand up to his chin, running it over his beard. 'Tell you what, then: when Ken does the cooking you're to help him. How about that?'

Zara grinned. 'That sounds like a very—diplomatic idea.' Then she gave him an innocent look. 'But perhaps it would be better if Ken continued to cook the captain's meals.'

'Oh—er—yes, I see what you mean.' Mack hesitated, but then shrugged. 'We'll see how it goes.'

He went back on deck and Tony said, 'I suppose I ought to start work.' But there was no enthusiasm in his voice. 'I'm supposed to clean out the bilges.'

'I've read about that; it sounds revolting.'

'It is,' Tony said feelingly.

'Well, it can wait for ten minutes. Have another cup of black coffee.' She poured it for him and one for herself. 'Tell me about the *Spirit of the Wind*,' she invited. 'How long have you been on it?'

'Her,' Tony corrected. 'Ships are always female.'

'And their crews love them more than their wives, I suppose,' Zara commented scornfully.

Tony grinned. 'Well, ships are always beautiful, but wives grow old and fat.' He ducked and laughed as Zara lobbed a spoon at him. 'I've only been on board a couple of months. We spent some time in France doing a commercial for French television, then we came on for this film assignment in Rhodes. I was at college before that.'

'What about the ship? What kind did you say it was when you showed me round that first time?'

'It's a fully-rigged three-masted ship. That means it has square sails on all three masts; that's the purest form of square-rigger,' he added on a note of pride.

'And it's a replica of an old ship; like a mock-Tudor house?'

'Better not let the skipper hear you say that,' Tony warned. 'This ship is the apple of his eye.'

A noise near the companion-way made them both look fearfully in that direction, but no one appeared and they gave a sigh of relief. 'Tell me about the skipper,' Zara invited. 'Has he been captain long?'

'He's been a ship's captain for some years, but not always on this ship. I think he sometimes captains other ships that belong to the company, and sometimes he's based in London for quite long periods. But I don't really know too much about it. You ought to ask Mack; he's the one who knows him best.'

'Thor Cameron,' Zara mused. 'It's an unusual name for an Englishman.'

'He isn't English. His father was a Scot and his mother was Danish.'

'Oh, I see. That accounts for it, then,' Zara re-marked, thinking about Thor's height and his fair hair with its hint of red.

But Tony said, 'For his confidence and authority, you mean?'

Zara supposed that Thor did have those qualities; most of the times she had seen him he had been so furiously angry that she hadn't had a chance to notice much else about him. 'Do you like him?' she asked curiously.

There was no hesitation in Tony's reply. 'Of course. He really knows his job and he's very fair. I know *you* don't like him, but a ship's captain has to be strict.'

'That shouldn't stop him from being human.'

'He is human—most of the time.' Tony grinned. 'Perhaps he's a misogynist.'

'I wouldn't be at all surprised,' Zara agreed feelingly. 'I take it he isn't married, then?'

'No, none of us are. Mack used to be married but his wife divorced him because he was away at sea most of the time.'

'Why didn't he give it up?'

Tony shrugged. 'The sea gets to you; it gets in your blood.'

'So that's why you're all so wet!'

He groaned. 'What a terrible pun to make when I feel so lousy.' Sighing, he got to his feet. 'I'd better change and get started on those bilges.'

Zara felt no inclination to offer to help him. She thought that he ought to have realised his drinks were being laced. Maybe he had; maybe he had secretly wel-comed an excuse to try to make a pass at her. It was working in nightclubs, Zara thought in annoyance; men always seemed to think that chorus girls had no morals. Maybe when she got back to England she'd start a movement: 'Girls Against Sexual Prejudice'—GASP. Yes, she rather liked that. She could imagine all the girls dressed in their show costumes, marching to Downing Street and carrying banners reading, 'DANCERS DEMAND RESPECT'. The thought made her giggle as she gazed into space, chin on hands, her elbows on the cluttered table.

It was at that moment, of course, that Thor chose to walk into the galley. His eyes swept over the place. 'I ordered you to keep this place clean,' he thundered. 'Not to sit mooning around like some lovesick teenager. Now jump to it.'

Zara was off the bench like a shot. 'OK. OK. Keep your hair on.'

He glared at her and stood watching as she began to clear the table and put the dishes in the dishwasher. Most of the mess had been made by Ken when he'd cooked—charred the breakfast and hadn't bothered to clean up afterwards. But there was no point in telling the skipper that, of course. He stood and watched her for a few minutes, then went over and poured himself a coffee, but pulled a face when he drank it. It was the last dregs of a pot Ken had made and was probably now so strong that it almost melted the cup. 'Can't you even make decent coffee?' Thor rasped, throwing it down the sink in disgust.

He left her to get on with her work, which Zara did willingly enough. The galley, luckily, wasn't also a replica of that in an old sailing ship; instead it had every labour-saving gadget, from a dishwasher through a washing-machine and tumble-drier to a microwave. There was also a fridge and a small freezer, with a much larger freezer down below in the dry store, along with more food and the spare sails. When she'd finished cleaning off all the burnt egg on the cooker Zara got down on her hands and knees and washed the floor. She was still kneeling down when Thor came back to check on her. He nodded approvingly; evidently he considered the position a suitably humble one for a woman.

The galley done, Zara consulted her list. The crew's cabins were to be cleaned and any dirty linen to be replaced and washed. Did that include the skipper's cabin? she wondered. Deciding that it would be better to keep well clear of Thor, Zara went to the two cabins in the front of the boat first. Not front, forward, she reminded herself. She must get used to the language of the ship and the sea. The cabins smelt extremely stale, to say the least. Zara threw open the portholes and took all the sheets and towels and what clothes she found lying around, and took them to be washed. Then she took the four sleeping-bags up on deck to air them.

Pete Keats, the Aussie, was at the helm and lifted an arm in a lazy greeting, and aloft, near the top of the main mast, Steve Johnson was keeping a look-out. The sky was devoid of clouds, the sea completely empty, without a sign of land or even of other ships. 'I expected the sea to be full of ships,' she remarked, going over to Pete, her arms full of sleeping-bags. 'There were always loads in Oran harbour.'

'They've got engines and can take a straight course; we have to sail with the wind currents.'

'How long will it take us to get to Rhodes?'

'About three weeks with fair weather and a good wind.'

Her eyes widened in surprise. 'As long as that?'

He mistook her exclamation for impatience. 'Don't worry, you'll soon be back on dry ground. We must be doing about five knots; that's good for the *Spirit*.'

Three weeks, Zara thought, lifting her face to the breeze. An ocean cruise in the sun. She could stand that without any trouble. But unfortunately there was bound to be trouble—in the large form of the skipper. And if he found her talking to Pete Thor would probably accuse her of trying to seduce him, too. Going down the deck, Zara looked for somewhere to hang the sleeping-bags to air. There was no obvious place, but she found a neatly coiled rope which she tied between two of the masts, doubling and twisting it so that the bags were caught between the loops and wouldn't blow away. After standing back to admire her ingenuity for a moment, Zara went back down below to finish cleaning the cabins.

It was almost an hour later when a bellow of rage reached every part of the ship. Zara recognised the skipper's voice and somehow knew instinctively that she was in trouble again. She was right; in less than a minute Mack came down and told her the skipper wanted her on deck. 'Now what?' she asked apprehensively, but Mack merely shrugged and gestured for her to go ahead of him. Zara looked at him suspiciously—she had an idea that he was trying very hard not to laugh.

Thor was pacing impatiently up and down the deck, and somehow most of the crew were also there, trying to look nonchalant. He swung round when Zara came up the companion-way and glared at her. 'What the hell are those?' he demanded, jerking a pointing arm to the line of bags.

Fed up with being continually got at, Zara decided to be obtuse. 'Sleeping-bags,' she said shortly.

Walking up to her, Thor put his hands on his hips and gave her a sardonic look. 'I know *what* they are. I——'

'Why ask me, then?' Zara got in.

'Watch it.' His eyes narrowed dangerously. 'I want to know what the hell they're doing on deck.'

'I should have thought that was obvious: they're airing.'

'Airing?'

'Yes. They smell. The cabins smell. In fact, this whole boat smells.'

'Ship,' Thor corrected as he stared at her, taken aback by her vehemence. Behind him a member of the crew laughed. Thor swung round. 'If you men haven't got any work to do I can soon find you some.' The men moved hastily away but managed to find things to do that were still within earshot. Thor's eyes went over them but he turned back to Zara. 'What exactly do you mean?'

'The cabins are musty.'

'Are you saying the men don't keep them clean?'

Conscious of the listening ears, Zara said, 'The cabins are small and can't be aired properly. And wet clothes have been left to dry in them. They need spring-cleaning, so that's what I'm giving them.'

'A woman's touch,' Thor said sarcastically.

'And what's wrong with that?' she retorted spiritedly.

'Nothing—I just didn't expect your kind of woman to have it. Not the *housewifely* variety, anyway.'

Zara's face flamed as she got his meaning. 'Do you have to insult me at every opportunity?'

'The kind of lifestyle you lead, what else do you expect?'

She felt the skin tightening on her face, but knew that she would do herself no good by arguing with him. But perhaps that was what he wanted. If he goaded her into a shouting match it would give Thor the excuse he wanted to lock her in her cabin all day long. So, curbing her justifiable anger, Zara said tightly, 'Do you want me to go on cleaning the cabins or not?'

The skipper regarded her for a moment and then nodded. 'Clean them, yes—but get these sleeping-bags and this damn washing-line off my deck. And don't turn it into a Chinese laundry again.'

'But how am I supposed to air them, then?'

He gave her an exasperated look. 'Use your initiative—and if that's too difficult for you, then see the first mate.' And he turned and went below, having successfully unloaded her on to Mack.

Going over to the bags, Zara began to take them down, her face set.

'I'll do the rope for you.' Mack came over, took the rope down and coiled it again. Now that Thor had gone below he was openly grinning.

'What's so funny?' Zara said sharply.

'Sorry.' Mack tried to look serious but couldn't. 'It was the look on the skipper's face when he saw the bags hung out on his deck like a load of washing.'

'I've an idea you're enjoying this,' she accused him.

'Well, you've certainly livened up the voyage so far— and you've only been aboard a couple of days.'

'And you can't wait to see what happens next,' Zara said sardonically. She felt resentful, but then remembered that Mack had intervened on Tony's behalf and realised that he must have a difficult position, always being between the crew and the captain. 'I thought ships had mixed crews nowadays,' she sighed.

'Some do, but the skipper always insists on an all-male crew now.'

'Now?' Zara gave him a curious look. 'He used to have mixed crews, then?'

The mate hesitated, but then nodded. 'He had a spot of bother in the past.'

'Really? What kind of bother?'

But Mack gave a vague shrug. 'I wasn't sailing with him at the time. You'd better get back below,' he advised.

Zara obeyed him, thinking that although he might not have been sailing with Thor he obviously knew all about his 'spot of bother'. A convenient phrase that could cover anything from a bad case of seasickness to—— Zara's mind boggled at all the possibilities. But, whatever it had been, the experience had obviously had a lasting effect on Thor if it had made him ban females from his ships forever more. Intrigued, Zara determined to find out what it had been. It might be possible to worm the story out of Mack, and, failing him, she could try some of the other men in the crew.

She finished cleaning the cabin she'd been working on, leaving it looking and smelling a whole lot better than before. All the clothes that had been left lying around had been stowed away, neatly folded, in the lockers, books and magazines put back on the shelves, shoes and boots placed in neat rows, and wet gear hung on coat-hangers.

Giving the cabin a look of satisfaction, Zara went back to the galley and began to prepare sandwiches for the crew's lunch, thick doorsteps of fresh bread and chunks of cheese. Ken came rushing in when she'd almost finished and gave a sigh of relief when he saw the piled plates of sandwiches. 'Oh, great. I was working in the engine-room and forgot the time. I'll take these through to the saloon.'

'Wait! You've got to do the skipper's lunch.'

'Aah.' He pulled a face. 'Can't you do it, Zara?'

'No. You know what we agreed.'

'Oh, OK. Here, give me the loaf.'

He began to cut off uneven wedges, the oil that lingered on his fingers staining the bread. He scraped the butter across and added a piece of cheese that must have weighed a quarter of a pound, then shoved it all on a tin plate.

'Is that it?' Zara stared at the 'sandwich' in disbelief. The ones that she had made were definitely man-sized but were delicate compared to Ken's concoction. 'Are your sandwiches usually like that?'

'I was in a hurry.' Grabbing up a can of beer and the plate, he said, 'I'll take these to the skipper,' and rushed out.

The members of the crew who weren't working on deck came down to find mugs and plates, and bowls of salad and various pickles laid out for them in the saloon. They tucked in appreciatively, forever hungry, Ken hurrying back to join them.

'Zara, if I were the skipper I would sign you on for life,' Arne Huss, the second mate, told her in his heavy Swedish accent.

They stayed in the saloon till it was time for them to go on watch, then she put out more sandwiches for the men who took their place. Tony was among these, looking a little better, but streaked with dirt from the bilges. Zara made him go and wash and change before he sat down, which he wasn't too pleased about, but she saved him some sandwiches so that was OK.

Leaving them to it, Zara went to clean out another cabin but passed the one that she'd just cleaned on the way—and stared in amazement. It was the cabin that Tony shared with Steve. In the short time since she'd cleaned it, Tony had dropped his dirty clothes on the floor, pulled everything out of his locker while looking for clean ones, rested his filthy hand on the white pillow, wiped his face on the clean towel, and for good measure kicked the shoes all over the floor. Her whole morning's work wasted. Zara stood dumb-struck in the doorway, then sighed and laughed to herself as she realised how typical it was of Tony to untidy it all again in minutes. Why was it that men, especially young ones, were always happier living in a mess?

'I thought you were supposed to be cleaning this cabin? It's a pigsty.'

Hardly able to believe her ears, Zara turned to find that the skipper had walked up behind her and was looking over her shoulder. 'I did clean it,' she said indignantly. 'It was fine until half an hour ago.'

'A woman's touch!' he repeated scornfully. 'Clean it up—and this time do it properly.'

He walked away, leaving Zara wishing she had something sharp to stick in his broad back. Damn him, she gritted under her breath. I'll show that arrogant, woman-hating swine. And, her temper seething, she set to and put the cabin to rights again.

It was all go that day; when she'd finished Tony and Steve's cabin she cleaned that of Mack and Arne, then her own, before having to stop to prepare the evening meal. But at least she worked out her anger and was glad to sit down with the others to eat. Thor's meal was thrown together by Ken and taken up to his cabin. Looking at it, Zara realised that she needed have no feelings for revenge when the skipper was forced to eat that kind of food every day.

When the crew weren't working they relaxed in the saloon. Zara finished clearing up the galley and went to join them, and found them playing poker. 'You wish to watch?' Arne made room for her on the bench.

'I'd like to play—but I don't have any money.'

'You can play poker?'

Zara smiled and nodded. 'It's amazing what you learn when you're waiting backstage between shows.'

'I lend you some money.' Arne pushed some coins towards her.

'But I can't pay you back if I lose.'

He shrugged. 'Maybe you'll be lucky.'

They dealt her in and Zara noticed that she and Arne were basically playing with Swedish coins, Pete with Australian, and Steve and Ken with British, but there was no bother about exchange-rates—they just tossed the coins in the kitty. Zara quite enjoyed playing cards, and she had learnt to watch people's faces when they played, to read their body language, so that she could often tell when someone was bluffing. Ken, she soon found, always rubbed his nose if he had a good hand, and Pete gave himself away every time by making his face go absolutely blank. Arne and Steve, however, were more seasoned players and it was difficult to tell with them. The stakes were very low, but gradually Zara began to win, and she eventually had quite a pile of money in front of her, over and above what Arne had lent her. Not that it mattered, because she couldn't possibly take their money, and intended to give it all back at the end of the game.

'You really *are* lucky!' Ken exclaimed after she'd out-bluffed him again. 'That's the fourth time you've done that.'

'Not really. It's because you always . . .' Her voice died away as she noticed that Thor had come into the saloon. He paused for a moment to watch them and then went into the galley. Zara heard the fridge door open and smiled inwardly, wondering if he was getting himself something decent to eat. She went to finish what she had been going to say, to tell Ken how he gave himself away, but a new hand was already being dealt and Ken was talking to Steve, so the moment passed.

Arne won the next hand, but in the following one Zara dealt out the cards and saw Ken rub his nose. She became absorbed in the game and didn't realise that Thor was standing a couple of feet behind her, watching the game over her shoulder. Again Ken threw in his cards and then groaned when he saw that she'd fooled him. 'It's uncanny!' he exclaimed. 'You beat me every time.' He looked at his dwindling pile of coins. 'If I don't start winning soon I'll be out of the game.'

'If you can't stand the heat get out of the kitchen,' Steve jeered. But he added, as Zara gathered in her winnings, 'That was some pot. You always seem to know when we have a good hand. You must be a very experienced player.'

Zara laughed. 'Not really. It's just that you and Ken are inexperienced. You see——' She broke off as a hand came down on her shoulder. Twisting her head, she saw Thor standing over her, his eyes contemptuous, the fingers that gripped her shoulder like steel.

'I want a word with you. Come up on deck,' he ordered shortly. Zara gazed up at him, the pack of cards still in her hands as she wondered what on earth was the matter this time. Reluctant to leave the security of the saloon, she opened her mouth to say 'why?' when Thor suddenly barked out, 'Move!' and she dropped the cards and got hurriedly to her feet.

He followed her up the companion-way, but when they reached the deck Thor took her arm and marched her up to the bow, away from the helmsman. It was a warm cloudless night, the stars bright diamonds against the velvet blackness of the sky, but Thor didn't even glance at the sky, he just swung her round to face him and said fiercely, 'It seems there is no end to your talents—if you can call them that.'

'I don't know what you mean,' Zara protested. 'And you're hurting my arm.'

'Good.' The grip tightened. 'I mean that you're a card-sharp as well as everything else.'

She gasped in surprise. 'Don't be ridiculous!'

'No? Then how come you win so often—and with a hand that no one in his right mind would bet on? And don't try to deny it; I was watching you.'

'I called Ken's bluff, that's all. He——'

'Liar! You dealt those cards and you knew what he had. You're nothing but a cheap little hooker and a cheat.'

'I am *not* a cheat,' Zara retorted furiously.

'You won't get the chance to be on my ship. You'll go back to the saloon and you'll give back every penny that you've fleeced out of the crew. And this will be your last card game, or any other kind of game or bet. Do you understand?' And he shook her arm angrily.

Her face flaming, Zara repeated vehemently, 'I am not a cheat!'

Thor laughed scornfully. 'Tell that to the marines! The sooner you get it into your head that you're not going to get away with your tricks and your lying on this ship, the better. You may be able to fool the crew but there's no way you can fool me.' He gave her a rough push. 'Now get below and give back that money—all of it. If you try to keep any I'll find it—and I can make you very sorry.'

It was useless to argue. Zara gave him a look of pure hatred, then turned and walked with as much dignity as she could on the rolling ship along the deck and down the companion-way. At its foot she stood for a minute, trying to regain some degree of calmness, but her voice was stiff as she went into the saloon and said, 'I'm tired. I think I'll turn in.' She pushed all her money back into the centre of the table. 'Here, divide this between you.'

'But we can't do that; you won it fair and square,' Pete protested.

'Yes, I know. But it's your money; I never intended to keep it. Goodnight.'

She turned away before they could argue any more, and took a shower before going to her cabin. After about ten minutes there was a sharp rap on the door. 'Yes?' But Thor didn't answer, he just turned the key in the lock and walked away.

Zara lay down on her bunk, convinced that this had been the worst day in her life. Ali Messaad had been a threat she had been desperate to run away from, but even he now seemed a whole lot less intimidating compared to Thor Cameron!

CHAPTER FOUR

FOR the next couple of days Zara managed to stay out of trouble simply by staying out of Thor's way. She learnt his routine from Tony and made sure she was always somewhere else. But every day, while they were at sea, he did an inspection of the ship. Accompanied by Mack, he went over the ship minutely, from the crow's-nest to the engine-room, making sure that all was in perfect order. His inspection included the cabins, the showers, and, of course, the galley, so he knew that Zara had been doing her allotted work, but she was as elusive as a ghost, disappearing up one companion-way as Thor came down the other. But evidently her work was satisfactory because he didn't start yelling for her again.

Pleased that she'd found a way to keep out of trouble, Zara was able to give her attention to a more pressing problem, that of her clothes—or, rather, lack of them. She had been able to bring so few things with her that she was permanently living in her jeans, which soon became grubby when she was doing so much cleaning, and which were also far too hot. Tony had given her a T-shirt so that she didn't have to wear her sweater all the time, and she had a change of underclothes, but having to wear the jeans was driving her mad. Zara looked enviously at the men in their swimming-trunks or shorts, their bodies cool and bronzed; even the skipper sometimes took off his white short-sleeved shirt while he was on deck, although he always wore crisp white shorts rather than the jazzy patterns favoured by the others.

One really hot day, Zara sweated so much as she worked that she began to get sore. Desperately she looked round for something else to wear—and came upon the flag locker. Rummaging around, she found one of the right size and it took no time at all to make it into a bikini bottom, the ends tied on her hips. The relief was tremendous. Zara gave a sigh of satisfaction and put her jeans into the washing-machine, although she wouldn't have minded just throwing them overboard.

She got a wolf-whistle from Pete when he saw her, but Tony and Steve, after giving her an appreciative look, made no comment; after all, they'd all seen her legs when she was in the floor-show back in Oran. Unfortunately, the next day Thor chose to do his inspection of the ship an hour earlier than usual and he and Mack walked into the galley while Zara was there. The cook's apron tied round her waist, Zara was preparing the vegetables for dinner. She turned to smile a greeting, but, taken by surprise at seeing the skipper, she dropped the opened bag of frozen peas she was holding, sending them sliding and scattering all over the floor.

Thor gave her the look he reserved for mindless idiots and clumsy women, then his eyebrows rose when she stood still, facing him. 'Well, don't just stand there, pick them up.'

'I'll—er—do it in a moment; I have to—to watch the water doesn't boil over.'

Thor's eyes narrowed. 'I said do it now. I don't want someone treading on those peas and breaking their leg.'

Zara nodded and edged away from him, but the cupboard containing the dustpan and brush was behind her and there was no way she was going to be able to reach into it without turning her back on Thor. Knowing there was no way to avoid another bawling-out, she sighed and turned to open the cupboard, bending down to pick up the things.

Behind her there was a momentary silence, and then Mack let out a great guffaw of laughter. Zara turned quickly to find Mack leaning against the wall, shaking with laughter, and even Thor had a huge grin on his face. He tried to wipe it off and look serious as she stared at them. His mouth worked as he strove to control himself, but then Thor turned abruptly and strode out of the galley. Mack quickly followed him and Zara stood in amazement, hearing both men's roars of laughter echoing through the ship.

Well! Completely disconcerted, Zara didn't know how to feel. She supposed she ought to be pleased that Thor hadn't had a go at her again, but she wasn't at all sure that she liked him laughing at her. Standing up, she tried to twist round to see what was so funny, but the bikini looked OK as far as she could see; not that she could see all that much. Cursing the lack of a full-length mirror on the ship, Zara went into the washroom where there were hand basins, with mirrors for shaving over them. She stood on a box with her back to the mirror and peered over her shoulder, but she had to get another box before she was tall enough. She was twisting round, trying to see her reflection, when Tony walked in.

'What on earth are you doing?'

'Can you see anything funny about my bikini?'

Puzzled but pleased, he came round to have a closer look. 'No, it doesn't look peculiar to me.'

'I don't mean funny peculiar, I mean funny ha-ha.'

Tony looked again. 'No, it's still OK to me.'

'Then why on earth——?' She broke off as the skipper came in.

His face became mask-like when he saw her on the boxes and she was sure he was trying not to laugh again. Tony, in a very cowardly manner, sidled out. Zara gave Thor an indignant look. 'What's so funny?' she demanded.

'Did you have to desecrate a flag by turning it into— that thing?' he demanded.

His words were harsh but his voice didn't match, and Zara was sure that he was having to fight his sense of humour. It was an unexpected surprise to know that he had one, of course, but she was too indignant at being laughed at to take advantage of it. 'It was all I could find. I had to have something to wear; I couldn't go around in those jeans any longer.'

His face changed, the amusement leaving his eyes. 'Don't you have any other clothes?'

'No. I had to leave all my things behind in Oran when I sneaked out of the hotel.'

'Because you hadn't paid your bill?'

Zara's face hardened. 'Because my handbag had been stolen and I couldn't get any money out of my account to buy a ticket home, as I've already told you.'

It was evident he still didn't believe her story, but Thor merely said, 'I'll see that some clothes are found for you. Can you sew?'

'Why, yes.' She went to climb down from her boxes and he automatically stepped forward and went to hold out a hand as if to help her down, but then he quickly stepped back again, leaving her to manage by herself. Turning, he went to walk away, but she said, 'Skipper,' and he paused in the doorway.

'Yes?'

'What was so funny?'

His lips twitched. 'You should learn to read signal flags,' he returned as he walked away.

An hour or so later Mack came into the galley carrying a small pile of things for her. 'The skipper sent these. There are a few clothes that might fit you, and some material for you to make new ones. And he says that you can use the sewing-machine that Arne uses to mend the sails. Get him to show you how.'

'That's great.' Zara took the things from him and began to go through them. Besides the lengths of material in white and blue, there were a couple of T-shirts with the name of the ship written on them, in a size small enough to fit her, a sarong—and, very strangely—a woman's sundress.

'The skipper said to alter the things if you need to.'

'OK, thanks. Mack? I take it you know how to read signal flags?'

Mack grinned. 'Yeah, but I'm not going to tell you.'

'Mack! That's not fair.'

He laughed openly. 'See Arne about using the machine.'

When he'd gone Zara took the things to her cabin, wondering where the sundress had come from. She tried it on but it was too big and would have to be taken in, but the sarong she tied round her waist and kept on in place of the bikini. Holding up the flag, she looked at it, twisting her head, trying to think what it could possibly mean, but she wasn't even sure which was the right way up.

Usually Thor ate alone in his cabin, but that evening he came to eat in the saloon with the crew. He must have had a go at Ken about burning his food, because tonight Ken gave him a pork chop so underdone that it was still bright pink. The rest of the crew tucked into a succulent beef casserole with jacket potatoes, followed by spotted dick and custard that Zara had made. For his dessert Thor got a tin of rice pudding.

Thor watched Zara as she dished out the casserole then went back to the galley to return with hot bread rolls and butter. Again she went back to the galley, but when she didn't return straight away he called out to her.

'Yes?'

She hurried in, fully expecting him to question her about the food, but he said, 'There's no place laid for you.'

'Oh, no. I usually eat when everyone has finished.'

To her amazement Thor said, 'You may have stowed away aboard the *Spirit*, but that doesn't make you a servant to the others. So long as you're on this ship you're a member of the crew and equal to the rest. Go and get a plate and sit down.'

Bemused, Zara said, 'Aye, aye, Skipper,' and went to obey him.

There was a space on the bench beside Thor, but when Zara came back she squeezed in between Tony and Pete. 'I have to be near the galley,' she explained for the benefit of anyone who cared to listen.

She had expected the crew to be intimidated by Thor's presence but they talked and ribbed one another just the same as they usually did. As they ate, Zara noticed that the ship was rolling more than normal, and she had to brace herself as she went round the table pouring the custard. Some spilt as the ship lurched and she looked quickly up at Thor, expecting him to tell her off for being clumsy, but he said nothing, his eyes going to the dish of rice pudding that Ken triumphantly put in front of him. You'd have thought that anyone could cook tinned rice, but even this Ken had managed to make into lumps.

Thor looked at it and pushed the plate away untouched. 'The wind's rising,' he said to Mack. 'We must be running into that storm that was forecast.'

'Want me to take over the helm, Skipper?'

'No, there's plenty of time. Finish your meal.' He watched as Mack poured a generous dollop of creamy custard over his second helping of pudding, then glanced at Ken. 'I take it you didn't make the custard,' he said drily.

Ken cleared his throat. 'Er—no. I let Zara make that— she needs the practice.'

A couple of the men choked on their food at that, and the rest tried to hide their grins. Thor gave Ken a sardonic look. 'It seems she's been "practising" quite successfully.'

Mack, tactful as always, changed the subject, asking the skipper if he knew yet what actors would be taking part in the film the ship was to be used for in Rhodes.

'The usual, I expect,' Thor returned. 'An up-and-coming juvenile and an aged has-been. That seems to be the norm for the male actors nowadays.'

'And the female?' Zara couldn't resist asking.

He shot her a look. 'I've no idea,' he said shortly. 'But I understand that they're going to make a few alterations to the ship to make her look like a sixteenth- rather than an eighteenth-century one. That will probably take a few days, and we'll have to keep a rigorous eye on their carpenters to make sure they don't do any damage.'

'What's the film about?' Zara asked curiously.

'The taking of Rhodes by Suleiman the Magnificent. But I think it mainly deals with the knights who were besieged within the fortress.' His glass slid across the table as the ship lurched, caught by a wave. He caught it neatly and stood up. 'If you'll excuse me I think I'll take a look on deck.'

The swelling sea made clearing up in the saloon and the galley after the meal almost into a game. Zara filled a tray with crockery, waited for the ship to roll in the right direction, and almost slid down into the galley, quickly setting the tray down before they rolled in the opposite direction again. The men who weren't on duty sat on in the saloon, but she noticed that Tony was starting to look a bit green.

'I thought there weren't supposed to be any storms in the Med,' he complained.

Mack laughed at him. 'This isn't a storm, this is only a slight swell. You should see some of the real storms in the Atlantic that this ship has weathered.' Standing up, he put a reassuring hand on Tony's shoulder. 'Don't worry, you'll soon get used to the movement.' He watched Zara do her trick with the trays and grinned. 'You look as if you've found your sea-legs.'

She laughed. 'It might have waited until I'd cleared the table.'

The ship rolled again, and Tony gave a groan and dived for the heads. Zara watched him go sympathetically. Never having been to sea before, she'd had no idea whether she would be a good sailor or not, but was very pleased to find that she evidently was. As soon as she'd finished clearing up she used the excuse of throwing a bucketful of scraps overboard to go up on deck. It wasn't quite night yet, but the sky was so grey and cloudy that it was almost dark. The wind was strong, making what sails were up crack like whips, but it wasn't raining and it wasn't cold.

As she came up on to the open deck the wind caught at Zara's hair, pulling it free of the couple of clips she'd used to keep it off her face, and sending it billowing in a silken mane around her head. The wind caught, too, at the skirt of the sarong, one minute lifting it above her knees, the next pressing it against the outline of her long, shapely legs. Not having enough hands to cope with everything, Zara concentrated on getting to the side with her bucket. Carefully she gauged the wind, then leaned over the rail to empty the bucket. But as she did so two hands came round her waist and yanked her back on to the deck. Unbalanced, Zara fell back into the man's arms.

For a moment she'd thought that it was Mack, but the height of the shoulder her head was leaning against made her realise it was Thor. He stood her up but kept a firm grip on her arm. 'You little fool! You could have gone overboard,' he shouted at her, his voice raised not only in anger but to be heard above the wind. Pulling her after him, he went down the main hatch and into the navigation-room, in between the galley and his own cabin.

He flicked on the light over the chart table, giving enough light to see but leaving the corners of the cabin in deep shadow.

'Haven't you got more sense than to lean over the rail in a stiff blow like this?' Thor demanded angrily. But then answered his own question. 'No, of course you haven't. I ought to have known you'd do something stupid like that. In future stay down below.'

'I can't stay down below all the time,' Zara protested. 'I need some fresh air.'

'Not in a storm you don't,' Thor snapped back.

'But you let the men come on deck.'

'That's different; they're part of the crew.'

Seeing her opportunity, Zara immediately said triumphantly, 'But at dinner tonight you said that while I was aboard this ship I was to be treated as a member of the crew and that I was equal to the others.'

'Just like a woman,' he said in angry contempt. 'Give her an inch and she demands a mile.'

'But it was what you said,' she insisted.

'That was as far as eating meals was concerned. Look, the men are trained how to behave on deck. They're taught to know every sail, every piece of rigging and equipment. They also know that they have to rope themselves to the ship during a storm. If you'd gone overboard you would have drowned,' he said brutally. 'There was no way we could have lowered a boat and found you in time in this sea.'

His face was grim, his eyes stern, and suddenly the storm wasn't a game any more. 'I'm sorry,' she said, meaning it. 'I was just trying to make sure that the scraps didn't fly back aboard in the wind.'

His eyebrows rose. 'Who taught you that?'

She grinned, the serious moment gone. 'Oh, I know all about sailing ships; I've read every one of the *Hornblower* books.'

Thor's mouth quirked in amusement, but he said, 'Then theory and practice are a couple of hundred years apart. You don't know the rules, Zara, so you must——'

'Then teach me,' she interrupted eagerly. 'Let me really be one of the crew. I don't get seasick like Tony. I could take his place on his watch, then you wouldn't be short-handed,' she urged persuasively.

But he gave a definite negative shake of his head. 'You're only a girl; you're not strong enough to withstand the wind, let alone pull on a rope. And besides,' he paused to emphasise his words, 'it wouldn't be worth training you; I'll be putting you ashore the moment we dock in Rhodes.'

The eagerness left Zara's face and her eyes fell. 'Yes, of course.'

She went to leave the cabin but Thor said, 'Zara?'

'Yes?' She lifted her head, half hoping that he had changed his mind, but he was looking at her with a mocking twist to his mouth.

'What happened to the bucket?'

'The buck...? Oh!' She flushed in annoyance. 'I—er—I think I must have dropped it overboard.'

The mockery increased. 'You see what I mean?'

Her anger rose. 'It was your fault. Being grabbed like that was enough to make anyone drop the stupid bucket.' Her chin rose. 'Take it out of my wages,' she said haughtily, but then spoilt the effect by adding waspishly, 'not that you pay me any, of course.' And she swept out of the cabin.

Four members of the crew were playing cards in the saloon, but tonight Zara didn't feel like joining them even if she'd been allowed to. Instead she went straight to her cabin and lay in her bunk, her mind as unsettled as the sea. She didn't really know why she'd asked Thor to let her train as a crew member, it had been an impulse thing. But she ought to have known that he'd say no, so she should have thought before asking. She was annoyed with herself for not doing so; she knew she often acted on impulse and was trying to overcome it—but the strange thing was that her impulses often turned out to be right for her. The ship heaved and Zara settled herself more comfortably in the hard bunk. Strangely, it made her remember the hardness of Thor's shoulder and the strength of the arms that had plucked her so easily back from the rail. Physically he was quite something, even though mentally he was just an extremely annoying MCP.

The storm increased during the night, and the next morning it was raining heavily. The men who came off watch into breakfast were wearing waterproofs, which they would have dropped on the floor if Zara hadn't yelled at them to go and hang them up in the shower area. Tony didn't put in an appearance and she found him lying in his bunk, feeling extremely sorry for himself and wishing that he'd never joined the ship. 'To think I could be at home with my mother looking after me and doing everything for me,' he said plaintively. 'She didn't want me to go to sea.'

'Aah, diddums,' Zara said unsympathetically. 'I bet you're an only child, too.'

He looked hurt. 'Well, yes, I am as a matter of fact. Are you?'

Zara nodded. 'Yes, unfortunately.'

Tony looked at her in surprise. 'I don't mind being an only child; although I suppose I am spoilt,' he added on a smug note. 'Would you have liked a brother or sister, then?'

'If it meant that my mother had someone else to take out her frustrated ambitions on, then yes, I would.'

'What about your father?'

'Oh, he walked out when I was still too young to remember him.'

Safe in the bosom of his doting middle-class family, Tony gave her a puzzled look. 'But—don't you keep in touch with him?'

Zara shook her head, knowing that he would never understand. 'No, I've never seen or heard from him

since.' Briskly changing the subject, she said, 'Now, are
you going to come and have some breakfast?'

Mention of food made him remember his queasy
stomach again and he groaned. 'Definitely not. I'm
staying here until this storm is over, and I'm getting off
this ship the second it reaches dry land.'

'You'll be here for a long time, then; I heard Mack
say he thinks it's going to go on for a week,' Zara teased
heartlessly.

She went about her work but was soon faced with a
problem. During the days she had been on board she
had thoroughly cleaned all the cabins that were being
used—except the captain's. She supposed that she was
meant to clean that, too, but somehow felt a reluctance
to do so. Apart from being a useful room in which to
bawl out the crew, Thor's cabin seemed a very private
place and one in which she didn't wish to intrude. But
obviously someone had to clean it, and as she was the
lowest of the low the task must fall on her. But Zara
couldn't just walk in and do it without permission. So,
instead of evading him as she normally did, she had to
go and seek Thor out.

He was up on deck, standing beside Arne at the helm,
his legs braced against the movement of the ship. Ropes
had been strung along the deck for the crew to attach
themselves to by a line, so that if they lost their footing
they wouldn't be swept overboard. Remembering yesterday's strictures, Zara clipped a loop of nylon line
round her waist and on to one of the ropes before ven-
turing on deck. She had borrowed Tony's wet-weather
gear and was clad in bright yellow from head to foot,
only her face and hands uncovered. For a few minutes
she stood on the open deck, gazing up at the swaying
sail-less masts that looked as if they might be torn away

by the force of the wind at any moment. The ship pitched and a great wave broke over the deck, almost sweeping her off her feet. Zara grabbed hold of the line and gave an excited laugh, loving every minute of it.

Dry and warm inside the wet gear, she turned to watch the grey angry sea, hardly able to believe that only two days ago this had been the intensely blue, placid mill-pond of a tideless inland sea. Now the waves broke fiercely against the ship, almost as if some malignant force was determined to batter it to pieces.

The ship had always seemed quite large before, but suddenly the *Spirit of the Wind* seemed very small and the sea very large and deep. Pushing away the thought of how many fathoms of water lay beneath them, Zara turned and bent against the wind as she made her way up to the helm.

'What is it?' Thor bent to shout into her ear, then gave an astonished gasp. 'Zara? What the hell are you doing up here?'

'I'm tied on to the line,' she pointed out.

He nodded. 'Yes. Good. What do you want?'

'Is it all right if I clean out your cabin today?'

'You came all the way up here to ask that?' He shook his head in wonderment. 'Yes, of course.' She nodded and went to turn away, but Thor reached out to stop her. 'Are you OK? You don't feel seasick?'

'No, I'm fine,' she shouted back, then suddenly gave him a brilliant smile. 'Isn't this great?'

His blue eyes widened, but then he nodded and grinned in return. 'Yes, but this is the other side of the coin.'

Thor's cabin was already meticulously tidy and he had very few personal possessions lying around; just the usual things in his private bathroom, and a few novels in the bookcase along with all the sailing manuals and sea stories. There were no photographs on display, and the only pictures on the walls were of sailing ships. A man in love with his work and obsessed by it, Zara presumed. Somehow it seemed very lonely. All of the other men in the crew had photographs of loved ones in their cabins, or, failing that, a few pin-up pictures to liven up the walls. Here, there was nothing personal, as if Thor had no other life. She wondered what he did when the *Spirit* was back in its home port of Bristol. Did he stay on board the ship—live on it? Or did he have a home ashore somewhere? Zara tried to imagine him living in Bristol but couldn't; somehow she could only picture Thor as she had just seen him, standing on the deck of the ship, seeing it safely through the storm.

Pulling her mind back to the job in front of her, Zara set to work, but this cabin was the easiest she'd had to clean and it didn't take her long, despite the rolling of the ship. She was on her knees, cleaning under Thor's bunk, when the ship lurched into the trough of a wave and the deck sloped so much that she rolled across the floor and ended up against the desk. She clutched at one of the drawer-handles to stop herself rolling back when the ship righted itself, but only succeeded in pulling the drawer right out, its contents spilling on to the floor.

Zara gave a gasp of dismay and quickly began to put the things back in the drawer; it would be just her kind of luck if Thor walked in right now and thought that she was going through his desk. Most of the things were commonplace: envelopes, notepaper, old ship's logs, but there was also a small pile of letters, some still in their envelopes. Picking them up, Zara couldn't help but notice that they were in a woman's handwriting, and those in the envelopes, addressed to Thor care of the owners in Bristol, bore a Danish stamp. Zara put the letters back in the drawer and the drawer in the desk, and got on with her work, but her eyes kept straying back as she wondered who the letters were from. Thor's mother was Danish, she remembered; most probably the letters were from her. Zara tried very hard to resist and almost overcame the temptation, but at the last moment simply had to go back and take a look at one of the letters. It was written in a foreign language that she could only presume to be Danish, and the signature was a sprawl that could have been anything, but definitely didn't look like 'Mother'.

The sound of voices as the watch changed made Zara hastily thrust the letter back with the others and grab up her cleaning tools. Her face flushed, she hurried out of the cabin, not looking round in case Thor was watching her, but when she reached the galley she glanced back and gave a sigh of relief when she saw that it was only Arne and Steve who had come off watch.

It was too early yet to prepare lunch. After glancing at her watch Zara decided to give herself a break and sat down with a mug of coffee. Her hands were shaking a little and her heart thumping. This is what it must feel like to commit a crime, she thought. She felt as if she'd committed one herself; ordinarily she would never have dreamed of looking at someone else's letters, wouldn't even have wanted to. But Thor was such an enigmatic figure, such a mystery, and she just longed to know what had happened to turn him into a woman-hater. But she was taken aback by her own audacity in looking at his letters; that was wrong, and she was rather afraid of the surge of curiosity that had made her do it.

The storm was blowing them off course, so Thor ordered the engines to be switched on, which meant that Ken was down in the engine-room. Zara made hot

sausage sandwiches for lunch and made Arne go back
on deck to tell the skipper that they were ready. Thor
came down below shortly afterwards and went to his
cabin before appearing in the galley. He was wearing a
polo-necked sweater over his shirt, the sleeves pushed
up, giving him an even more nautical air. Looking at
him, Zara decided that he could never be anything else
but a sailor. He fitted the part so exactly, as his Viking
ancestors had done down the ages.

Tony hadn't put in an appearance for lunch, which
meant that he must still be feeling ill; nothing else would
keep him from his food. Ken was down with his beloved
engines, Arne and Steve had gone to rest, and Mack and
Pete were on deck, steering the ship. Thor ate his
sandwich with enjoyment and Zara didn't interrupt him
until he'd finished, then said, 'Would you like another?'

'Please. You make good sandwiches. And you made
a good job of cleaning my cabin. Thanks.'

Zara's hand shook again and she almost dropped the
sausages, but luckily she was standing with her back to
him so Thor didn't see the flush of colour that sped to
her cheeks.

'Did—did the forecast say how long the storm would
last?' she managed to ask.

'At least another twelve hours. It's unusual to have
one last so long in this area, but the weather has been
haywire this summer.' He grinned. 'But it's true about
an ill wind—at least this will keep the cruise ships in
harbour.'

'Don't you approve of cruise ships?'

Thor gave a definite snort of derision. 'They're just
floating hotels and casinos, with people eating themselves sick and the women dressing to kill when they

have their photograph taken at the captain's cocktail party.'

Zara smiled at his description as she turned the sausages over. 'I take it you wouldn't want to captain one, then?'

'God forbid! Give me a sailing ship every time.'

'We're using the engines at the moment,' Zara pointed out, tongue in cheek.

But Thor recognised the slight note of mockery and his eyes crinkled in amusement. 'So we are, at that. But we're already late for our appointment in Rhodes and needs must when there's a wind like this blowing us off course. How's Tony?'

'Getting better. I think he must have eaten something that disagreed with him,' Zara said tactfully.

'You mean he's as sick as a sea-dog,' Thor said shortly. 'And wishing he'd never boarded this ship, I imagine. I'll go and take a look at him later; it's about time he was routed out and got back to work. I need three people in each watch.'

'I could stand his watch for him,' Zara said eagerly, but then could have bitten her tongue. She knew what Thor's feelings were on the subject, so all she'd done was to lay herself open to another chauvinistic telling off.

She put his sandwich on the table, her eyes lowered, but Thor gave her an intent look. 'You're really keen, aren't you?' But then he shook his head. 'I've known girls who were keen before, but they never lasted the course; they were always getting side-tracked.'

'Oh? How?'

He flashed her a sardonic look. 'They were always falling in love, or flirting with the men and creating bad feeling among the rest of the crew.'

'Is that why you won't have women on board?'

'One of the reasons.'

Zara wondered what the others were, but said, 'If I guarantee not to flirt and not to fall in love, will you let me take Tony's place until he's better?'

Thor laughed shortly. 'As if any woman could guarantee that! No, I'm having Tony out of his bunk shortly.'

But, when he'd finished eating and went to look at Tony, Thor called Zara and made her bring the ship's first-aid kit. 'He's got it badly,' he told her when she returned. 'I'll give him an injection that should help, but he'll have to stay in his cabin until we're out of this blow.' Taking a syringe from the kit, Thor filled it and then gave Zara a doubtful glance. 'Think you can help me?'

'Yes, of course.'

'OK, hold Tony's arm steady while I give him the injection.'

Tony was too ill to care any more and let her hold his arm down while Thor knelt down to swab it and find a vein; a tricky enough job when the ship was rocking so badly.

'Come on, old son.' Thor's touch and manner were surprisingly gentle. 'We'll soon have you back on your feet.' The needle slid into Tony's arm and Zara felt her face go white, but she gritted her teeth and didn't turn away. 'Well done,' Thor congratulated, but whether it was her or Tony he was complimenting she wasn't sure; perhaps it was both of them. He stood up. 'Wrap him up and keep him warm, and a drop of brandy won't do him any harm. I'm going to the navigation-room to plot our position and get the latest weather forecast.'

Zara did what she could for Tony and gave him a swig of brandy from the bottle she'd seen beside the medicine chest in Thor's cabin. On the way back she glanced in the navigation-room, but the skipper had already gone back on deck.

It was so exhausting on deck that the watches were reduced to two hours on and two off, but when Mack and Pete came off watch they just had a mug of coffee, liberally laced with rum, and went straight to their cabins to sleep. Zara made a tureen of very thick, spicy soup which the men could help themselves from as they wanted it, but aside from that had little to do. Apart from the terrible sound of the waves breaking against the ship and the creaking groans of the stout timbers of the hull, the ship was relatively quiet. Zara moved around, periodically checking on Tony, making sure there were warm towels ready when the men came below, doing what she could. The navigation-room was next to the galley, and she thought she heard a noise coming from it. A light was flashing on the radio set and it was giving off a loud buzzing noise. Knowing nothing about the radio, her first thought was that possibly there was another ship in trouble somewhere and it was sending out an SOS signal.

Quickly she ran and got a bleary-eyed Mack out of his bunk. Not having the captain's preconceptions about women, Mack snapped out, 'Go and get the skipper.'

Zara hastily pulled on Tony's waterproofs again and went out on deck. The sky was so grey now that it was completely dark. Rollers swept across the deck continuously, impatient of the fragile ship in their path, and the only light was that from the ship's own masthead lanterns. Thor had climbed a few feet up the mainmast, but came down when he saw her.

'Mack sent for you,' she yelled at him. 'Somebody's trying to get through on the radio.'

'All right.' He glanced at Pete at the helm and gave her a rather helpless look. 'I can't leave Pete alone,' he shouted. 'Will you stay with him?'

She nodded her head vigorously. 'Shall I go up the mast?'

'Good God, no! Just stay with him in case he needs to send for me. I won't be long.'

He ran back down the deck, confident of his footing even though it heaved under him. Zara stood beside Pete, securely attached to the rope and keeping her balance by holding on to the mizen-mast. It was impossible to keep a proper watch from the deck; one minute they were on the crest of the sea, the next the ship was falling at what seemed to be an angle of ninety degrees and crashing down into the trough of the waves. Impossible not to be afraid in such a sea, but somehow it was exhilarating too. Zara clung to the mast and held her breath as they went sliding down towards the bottom of the sea, only to miraculously rise and do it all over again.

A great wave suddenly hit them and poured over the deck. Pete lost his footing and went crashing against the side, the wheel flying from his hands. It spun round as fast as a roulette wheel, the ship yawing and turning. Zara made a grab at it and got a bang on the shoulder before she managed to catch hold of one of the spokes. But even that wasn't much good because she didn't know which way to turn the thing. 'Are you all right?' she yelled at Pete.

He got slowly to his feet, obviously dazed, and managed to sway over to her, holding his arm against his chest. Between them, he using his left arm and Zara both of hers, they managed to bring the ship round on course again.

Within two minutes Thor was back on deck. He summed up the situation and immediately sent Pete below. 'I'll take the wheel.' He gave Zara a grim look. 'I'm afraid I'll have to ask you to stay here with me.'

She brushed stinging spray from her eyes. 'Was it an emergency on the radio?'

'Yes, but another ship is dealing with it. We can stay on course.'

Zara nodded and took up her position on his left side, where she only had to turn her head to see his strong profile as he faced the storm, fighting it, his feet braced, his powerful shoulders turning the wheel to his will. A strange, surely misplaced feeling of contentment came over her, and Zara smiled as the storm continued to rage about them.

CHAPTER FIVE

THE storm seemed to give one long, fiercely vindictive blast, and then suddenly lessened as if all its strength was spent. The rain stopped, and they could hear the sound of the ship's engine again, chugging solidly on. The grey skies lightened a little, though it was almost evening and they soon grew dark again, but this time the night was clear and they could see the stars.

'We've weathered it,' Thor said with satisfaction as he looked up at the sky. 'Go below, will you, and tell Mack to send a couple of men up to set the sails? And tell Ken he can switch off the engines.'

'Aye, aye, Skipper.'

Zara went to unhitch the line round her waist, but Thor said, 'Better keep it on; the deck's still slippery. And, Zara...'

'Yes?' Putting her hand on the mast, she turned to face him, but first had to wipe away the salt spray that clung to her eyelashes.

'You've done well,' he said almost roughly. 'Stay below and get some rest; you must be tired.'

'So must you,' she pointed out. 'You haven't slept since the storm started.'

He shrugged, the movement almost lost beneath his oilskins. 'I'm used to it. Ask Mack to check on Pete and let me know how he is.'

'OK.'

Zara found she was glad enough to go below; the storm had stimulated her senses, but now it was over she felt drained of energy and stumbled a little going down the companion-way. She found Mack in the navigation-room, sitting in front of the radio.

'Did the ship that was in trouble get rescued?' she asked.

He nodded. 'The crew had to abandon ship but a cargo ship picked them up. Does the skipper want me?'

'Yes, he wants you to send a couple of men to put the sails up. And he wants to know how Pete is.'

'He's hurt his arm; I'm not sure whether it's broken or not—we'll just have to wait until we get to Rhodes to find out, I suppose.'

'But that's terrible! You ought to have a doctor on board,' Zara exclaimed.

Mack laughed at her. 'There aren't enough doctors for every ship that goes to sea.' Switching off the radio, he went to find someone to help him put up the sails while Zara pulled off her wet gear and went to give Ken the skipper's message.

In the galley the soup had all been eaten, the pan left empty on the cooker, but at least there was some coffee left in the percolator. Zara poured some and drank it quickly, immediately feeling better. She checked on Tony and Pete and found them both asleep, the latter with his left arm strapped up in a sling. Tony, she imagined, would start to feel better now that the storm had died, but Pete's arm would be a constant worry for him until he could have an X-ray to make sure it wasn't broken.

Stirring herself, Zara cooked some ham and eggs with hot rolls and took it along to Thor's cabin. When she knocked his 'Come in' sounded impatient and weary. He was sitting at his desk, writing up the ship's log, his eyes red-rimmed, his shoulders sagging with fatigue.

'I thought you'd be hungry. You haven't eaten since lunchtime.'

His brows rose in surprise. 'Thank you. That was— thoughtful of you.'

He made room on his desk and Zara leaned past him to put the tray down. He must have showered; he smelt fresh and clean and his fair hair shone. Zara felt a sudden, stupid desire to touch him, to smooth back the lock of hair that fell forward on to his forehead, to run her fingers across the softness of his lips.

She stood back abruptly, shaken by her own feelings, balling her hands into tight fists at her sides. 'Tony and Pete are asleep.'

'Yes, I know; I looked in on them. Did you?'

Zara nodded, and swallowed, her throat dry. 'Well, goodnight, Skipper.'

'Goodnight, Zara—and thanks again.'

For the meal? she wondered as she walked back to her own cabin. For staying on deck in the storm? But he certainly wouldn't thank her if he'd known of the surge of desire that had so shaken her. It was loneliness, she thought desperately, or because he looked so weary. Yes, that was it, it was her maternal instincts coming to the fore. But a moment later Zara realised that there had been nothing in the least maternal about that sudden surge of emotion.

She fancied him. Her libido had risen to slap her in the face and draw her to the one man who definitely wasn't interested. Sod's law. Of all the crew, Pete was probably conventionally the best-looking, with his dark hair and eyes, but it was Thor's rugged handsomeness that had turned her on. But maybe not; maybe it was his unapproachableness that attracted her, the way a woman playing hard to get attracted a man, so Thor's

woman-hating attitude might have intrigued her. Perhaps
it was his dislike and abruptness to her that provoked a
challenge to her female sexuality. Zara gave a deep sigh
as she climbed stiffly into her bunk. A mere challenge
to her femininity she could fight and subjugate, but if
it was real desire... She fell immediately asleep, Thor's
image in her mind.

The next morning the sky was a cloudless azure blue,
the sea as calm and placid as if the storm had never
been. Zara slept deeply and didn't wake until the sun
shining through the porthole of her cabin touched her
face. Her first thought was for the crew's breakfast, but
when she quickly dressed and went into the galley she
found Mack there, frying some eggs.

'I'm late. I'm sorry.'

'No problem,' he said easily. 'We each got our own
breakfast this morning. You all right?'

'Yes, of course.'

He nodded. 'The skipper was pleased with the way
you handled yourself yesterday. He told me to tell you
that you can go on deck whenever you want.'

'Really?' Zara's face lit. 'That will be—nice,' she said
inadequately.

'Want some eggs?'

'Please. But what about Tony and Pete?'

'They're still in their cabins; you can make some
breakfast for them after.'

But Tony emerged from his cabin like some butterfly
miraculously emerging from a chrysalis, his stomach
back to normal now that the storm had died, and eager
to make up for all the meals he'd missed. Mack went to
give Pete a hand to get dressed and he, too, came into
the saloon for his breakfast.

'How's the arm?' Zara asked him.

'I guess I'll live,' he answered in his Aussie drawl. 'It doesn't hurt too much, so I don't think it's broken, but the skipper said to keep it strapped up and not use it, just in case.' He grinned. 'So I guess I'll just lie out on deck and sunbathe for the rest of the trip while you cobbers do all the work.'

He got the derisive remarks he deserved for that and they were all laughing when Thor came into the saloon, his step brisk, and with no sign of last night's weariness. He smiled when he saw that both Tony and Pete were there. Zara had braced herself to see him again, determined not to feel any emotion whatsoever; not sympathy, not misplaced desire, not curiosity. And she managed to hold on to her resolve—for about thirty seconds, until he smiled; then her heart gave a great lurch and she had to quickly turn and pretend to be busy at the cooker in case anyone saw her face and recognised the emotions there.

That morning Zara kept herself busy with all her chores, and then borrowed Arne's sewing-machine to take in the sundress and make herself a halter-top and matching shorts out of some of the material Thor had given her. After lunch, wearing her new clothes, Zara went up on deck. All the sails were set and the ship was dancing across the sea, the breeze carrying her speedily along. The deck planking had been washed clean of the salt left by last night's waves, and sparkled in the sun. Ropes had been recoiled, rigging repaired, and brass burnished, so that the *Spirit* looked like a new and shiny ship. The crew, too, had a light-hearted spirit today; they were all on deck, seated near the helmsman, doing hand jobs if they were on duty, sunbathing if they weren't, happy that they had weathered the storm with so little damage and hurt.

Mack saw Zara at the companion-way and waved her over. 'Make room for Zara,' he ordered. He was mending a frayed rope, his fingers agile.

The eyes of the men ran over her and some lingered for a while, especially Tony's, but they soon got used to her and treated her like another crew member. They all knew of her help in the storm and it had somehow made her one of them. 'What are the different sails called?' she asked idly, and immediately had half a dozen experts ready to give her a lesson.

'The only way to teach her is to take her round the ship,' Mack pointed out. So Steve and Tony gave her a guided tour, teaching her the names for the sails and masts. Zara tried to take it all in but got thoroughly confused by main royal topgallant, jigger staysail, and spanker.

'You're kidding me!' she exclaimed when she heard the last name.

'Now would we kid you?' Steve demanded in a hurt tone.

'Yes, you definitely would. I don't believe you.'

'For once he wasn't kidding.' Thor's voice behind her made Zara quickly turn. 'It really is called a spanker.'

'The names all sound so confusing,' Zara murmured.

'They're easy enough once you get used to them. It would probably help if you saw a plan of the sails. I think I've got one in my cabin, if you're really interested.' There was a doubtful, questioning note in his voice.

'Yes. Thank you, I'd like to see it.'

He nodded, then said, 'Can you spare me a minute?'

It was a politely worded order, but an order nevertheless. After thanking Steve and Tony, who nodded and walked away, Zara turned to Thor. 'Yes, Skipper?'

He began to walk up to the bow and she fell in beside him. 'Tell me again exactly what happened to you back in Oran.'

She blinked, wondering why, and why now. They reached the bow of the ship and came to a halt. Quickly she repeated the story, her voice matter-of-fact, her eyes looking steadily out to sea instead of searching his face for his reaction.

When she'd finished Thor made no comment about whether he now believed her or not, but said briskly, 'I want you to write down all the details about your bank account and credit card that you can remember; and the date on which your bag was stolen. Did you report it to the police?'

Zara shook her head. 'There didn't seem to be much point. The Arab who was interested in me was an important official in the town.'

'Well, let me have all the details you can remember.'

'Yes, OK. But why do you want it all now instead of when we get to Rhodes?'

'So that I can radio the details ahead to the authorities there, and with any luck you might have a new credit card waiting for you as well as your passport by the time we arrive. Even if there isn't it will have helped to expedite the procedure.'

So that he can get rid of me all the sooner, Zara thought unhappily.

But Thor was saying, 'And, speaking of your next of kin, it occurs to me that your parents won't know that you've left Oran or where you are, and will probably be worrying about you. So if you give me your home address I'll see that a message is sent to them via the radio.'

Glancing over the side, Zara could see the crest of the bow wave coruscating in the sun before it broke away into a long, rippling wake.

When she didn't answer at once Thor said, 'Zara?'

She turned to face him. 'It's very kind of you to offer, but there's really no need to send a message.'

'You have no parents?'

'Oh, yes—well, at least, I have a mother. But she—I think it will be best to wait till we get to Rhodes before I contact her.'

'Won't she be worried if she doesn't hear from you?'

Zara's mouth drew into a grim line. 'The only time she'll worry is if she thinks I've given up dancing,' she said shortly. 'She'd rather I was back in Oran, dancing, under *any* circumstances, than here.'

Thor's blue eyes ran over her set face and he didn't attempt to question her any further. 'All right. But if you change your mind you only have to let me know; it isn't difficult to send a message.'

He spoke dismissively, but Zara didn't want this first natural conversation she'd ever had with him to end there, so she said quickly, 'I suppose you get to travel all over the world?'

She was afraid he might snub her, but Thor said, 'Yes, I think I've been to most places.'

'On this ship?'

'This and others.'

'But you're based in England?'

'Yes, in Bristol.' He smiled slightly. 'That's what the ship and I call home.'

'I thought you might live in Denmark,' Zara remarked, trying to keep her voice light. 'Somebody told me you were half-Danish.'

Thor put his arms on the rail and looked out at the horizon. 'Yes, my mother was Danish, but I've never lived permanently there.'

'Was?'

'Yes, she died nearly ten years ago.' He straightened up. 'Let me have those bank-account details as soon as possible.'

'Yes, of course. I mean—aye, aye, Skipper.' Zara turned and went down below to do it at once.

Finding a pen and paper, she seated herself at the table in the empty saloon and began to write, but presently her hand became still as she gazed unseeingly down. If Thor's mother had died that long ago then the letters she'd seen in his cabin, which were dated only last year and the year before, couldn't possibly be from her. Perhaps they were from another relation? Or from a former girlfriend? Zara felt such a sharp stab of jealousy at the thought that it startled her. Hey, this wouldn't do! Disturbed by her own feelings, she bent to start writing again and found that she'd written Thor's name alongside her own.

After that, Zara tried to avoid Thor for completely different reasons. Instead of handing him the information he'd asked for, she left it on his desk. When he did his rounds she was in another part of the ship, and she only went on deck when he was down below. But there was no avoiding him when he came to the saloon to eat with the crew that evening. Everyone now knew that it was Zara who was doing the cooking, and Ken made only a token pretence by putting some of the food she'd cooked on to Thor's plate in the galley and taking it out to him.

Thor's eyebrows rose when he saw it wasn't burnt, and he licked his lips appreciatively at the taste. 'You're improving,' he said to Ken wryly.

'It's just practice, Skipper,' Ken said cheerfully.

Thor gave him a sardonic look. 'And tuition, I think.'

'Don't knock it, Skipper,' Mack advised. 'Just be thankful it's edible.'

There was plenty of room at the table when Zara came to join them, but Thor gestured to the bench at his side. Slowly, carrying her plate, Zara slid into the place alongside him. Reaching into his pocket, Thor produced the plan of the ship's sails that he had promised her. 'You see,' he pointed out, 'it's really very simple. You just have to remember which mast is which, then add the names of the sails. So you have fore royal, main royal, and mizen royal, and so on.'

'But what about this one?' Zara objected. 'It's called a crossjack.'

'Ah, yes.' Thor gave her a sudden grin. 'Unfortunately you've spotted the only exception to the rule. Technically it should be called the mizen course, but it's always known as the crossjack.' He looked round the table. 'Does anyone know why?'

Everyone shook their heads, but it led to a discussion on terms used at sea. Knowing nothing about the subject, Zara couldn't join in but she enjoyed the conversation, the friendly atmosphere, the feeling that she was accepted now. And she tried very hard not to notice Thor's nearness or to let her hand tremble when it accidentally touched his as they both reached for the bread basket.

'Sorry.' Thor glanced at her but Zara quickly turned her eyes away.

Trying to think of something to say, she looked rather desperately round the table and came up with, 'Your beards are all getting really long. I wonder what you'll look like when you shave them off at the end of the voyage.'

'What makes you think we're going to shave them off?' Pete asked her. 'I'm going to keep mine.' He stroked his hand over his admittedly attractive beard. 'Girls always go for a man with a beard.'

'I can't see my mother letting me keep mine,' Tony remarked, and got a lot of ribald remarks about being a mother's boy in return.

Maybe that's happened to me, Zara thought eagerly. Maybe I've just fallen for Thor because he has a beard. But every other man on the ship had a beard and she hadn't fallen for any of them. Tentatively she said to him, 'Do you always have a beard or have you just grown it for the film?'

'No, I've had one for years.'

Without thinking, she said, 'I wonder what you'd look like without it.'

Thor's eyebrows rose a little and he chose not to take the question as a personal one. 'Very odd, I imagine. With one half of our faces tanned and the other not.'

Ken said, 'I'm going to shave mine off immediately after the film. My girlfriend says they make men look older.' He turned to Zara. 'What do you think?'

'I haven't seen you without one,' she protested.

'No, I mean men in general.'

She looked round the table from man to man, her eyes coming last to Thor's face, his blue eyes amused, as they all waited in silent expectation for her verdict. She looked at him for longer than she should have done, but then blinked and said lamely, 'I suppose it depends on the chin behind the beard.'

They groaned at that and teased her about being tactful. Zara laughed, but as the conversation changed she became quiet, hardly hearing what was said. Her thoughts were full of the man beside her; she was very aware of his closeness, of the width of the shoulder that often brushed hers, of the scar that ran across the back of his right hand, a hand that looked to be too fine to be that of a seaman, for all its strength; of his voice, firm and deep, and the sheer masculinity of him.

Thor left the saloon after dinner and didn't come back. Zara played cards—but not for money—with those men not on duty, but somehow the evening had become tame and she pleaded tiredness to go to bed early.

Most of the crew wore a 'uniform' of T-shirts and shorts, things that got washed but never ironed. Thor and Mack, however, as the only officers, always wore white shorts, and their shirts, which they mostly only wore in port or in the evenings, were also white, with short sleeves and epaulettes on the shoulders to which they attached their badges of rank. These, together with knee-high white socks, white shoes, and their uniform caps, made them look very smart. Except when Tony was given the job of washing and ironing the officers' clothes. He somehow managed to mix them up with something else so that they came out pale blue, and ironed them so badly that the creases were in all the wrong places. He came looking for Zara, his face a picture of woe.

'Look at these! I can't give them back to Mack and the skipper like this.'

'You should have washed them by themselves.'

'I thought I had, but someone had left a navy-blue towel in the machine and I didn't notice it.' He gave her his best 'little boy lost' look. 'Can you help me, Zara?

The skipper will want his clean uniform for the service tomorrow.'

'Well, you'll just have to wash them all over again, and even then it might not come out unless you use a bleach solution. You'll have to be careful, though, that you don't ruin them completely.'

'I'm bound to. Couldn't you do them for me? Please, Zara. After all, I did help you to stow away on board.'

Zara gave him a grim look. 'So you did. All right, I'll do them for you, but I'll consider it to be a complete repayment of what I owe you, so don't try emotional blackmail again, OK?'

Tony grinned, instantly happy again. 'Thanks, Zara, you're a doll.' And he kissed her on the cheek before thrusting the pile of garments into her arms.

'Men!' Zara muttered as she watched him go jauntily away.

It took her several hours of delicate work before she got the clothes back to their original pristine white, and it was gone midnight before she had carefully pressed them, hung the things on hangers and could take them along to Mack's and Thor's cabins. Mack was up on deck, taking the watch, and it was easy just to leave his clothes in the cabin he shared with Arne, but Thor's cabin door was shut and he was evidently inside. Which was awkward if he wasn't to know that Tony hadn't done the job he'd been given. Zara hesitated at the door, wondering what to do. She couldn't see any light underneath, so presumably the skipper was asleep; and there was no way she wanted to wake him. Having cleaned the cabin, she knew the layout and remembered that there was a hook on the back of the door. If she opened the door just a little it should be possible to slip her hand inside and hang the clothes on the hook. Reaching for the knob, Zara slowly turned it and quietly eased the door open.

The cabin wasn't quite dark; the curtains were undrawn, letting the moonlight shaft through the windows across the sleeping figure in the bed. Holding her breath, Zara felt for the hook but found that it was further in than she could reach. Grimacing, she pushed the door wider and tiptoed inside. The light came on and Thor sat up in bed, all in one movement. Zara gave a small shriek of fright and whirled to face him.

'What the hell are you doing, creeping about in here?' Thor demanded.

'I'm sorry; I didn't want to wake you.' Zara edged towards the doorway, clutching the hanger in both hands, her eyes large in her face as she saw that the blankets had dropped low on his hips and it was made evident that the skipper didn't believe in pyjamas.

'Wait!'

His peremptory command held her still, but she could feel her cheeks going beetroot-red.

'Come in; close the door.' Thor became aware of his nakedness. 'And then—er—turn your back,' he ordered. Zara did so, there was the sound of movement behind her and then he said, 'OK, you can turn round.'

He had pulled on a pair of jeans which he was buckling round his waist. The skin of his chest was smooth and hairless, the strength in the muscles of his shoulders, arms, and broad chest emphasised by the lamplight.

'All right; what are you doing, sneaking in here in the dark?' he demanded again, his face grim.

Zara held out the hanger, her hand unsteady. 'I—I brought you your clean uniform.'

'Why you? I gave the job to Tony to do.'

'Yes. Well—er—he's busy at the moment, so I brought it.'

'At this time of night?'

'Well, we knew you wanted it for the morning, you see.'

Thor was studying her face. 'And Tony thought I might bawl him out if it wasn't here and ready on time? Is that why he sent you?'

'Oh, no. He doesn't know I——' Zara broke off, realising the pit she was walking into. 'That is, he asked me to bring the uniform earlier but I forgot.'

The skipper gave her a shrewd look. 'Or did he forget to bring it himself so you brought it along to try to get him out of trouble?' He gave a short laugh. 'You obviously have a soft spot for Tony. All right, leave the uniform. And don't try sneaking in here ever again. A lifetime at sea has taught me to be a very light sleeper, so I'll always hear you. OK, get going.'

'Yes. I'm sorry. G-goodnight.' Zara got out of the cabin fast and ran back to her own, but the incident must have set her adrenalin going, because somehow that night she just couldn't get to sleep.

The next day, Sunday, Thor held the service out on deck for those who wished to attend. It was very much a non-denominational affair so most of the crew usually went along, as much for the change in routine as anything else. Today, though, the word had gone round that Tony had made a hash of washing Thor's uniform and they were all looking forward to see what would happen; would Thor wear last week's crumpled uniform or would he appear in a fetching shade of blue? So when he came out on deck with his clothes white and crisp there were several whistles of surprise and boos of disappointment. Thor's left brow rose, his eyes swept round them, rested for a moment on Zara, whose chin came up even though her cheeks had coloured a little, and settled on Tony, who was looking fixedly at the deck. A sardonic look came into Thor's eyes but he went straight into the service.

He's guessed, Zara thought as she stood with the others, their heads bent reverently. He only had to take one look at us and he knew. It was disturbing to think that he could so easily read their faces, especially the way she was feeling about him. Angrily, Zara wished her feelings for him would hurry up and pass. Maybe if she had a flirtation with one of the others it would take her mind off Thor and the attraction would melt away, she thought hopefully. But when she reviewed the other men in her mind Zara found that she hadn't the smallest wish to flirt with any of them, however mildly. Besides, it might not be taken so mildly by the man she picked on, and she had this strange abhorrence of Thor finding out and having his worst ideas about her confirmed.

The prayers over, they all lifted their heads to sing the hymn 'For those in peril on the sea'. Most of the men had sung the hymn so many times that they knew the words off by heart, but Zara had to read them from a service sheet Mack had given to her. Some of the men could sing quite well, and those who couldn't thought that good singing meant raising their voices very loudly, so Zara, who had a very good voice when she wanted to use it, was quite drowned out.

A hand nudged her in the back, and Tony, who had edged behind her, sang into her ear in tune with the hymn, 'What do you think will happen about the uniform?'

Zara gave a small shrug, in annoyance as much as in reply. She looked up to where Thor was facing them all,

so tall that he had no need of a box to stand on to make
himself seen. He had taken his cap off for the service
and his fair hair was caught by the breeze. He looked
as his Viking ancestors must have looked so many cen-
turies ago, his skin tanned by the sun, his eyes as clear
blue as the sea he loved. A great ache filled Zara's heart;
it seemed to grow until it filled her chest and threatened
to burst out of her body. The ache spread, filling her
veins, reaching deep into her soul. Her hands began to
tremble and her voice died as she stared at Thor, her
eyes wide and strangely afraid. His eyes met hers for a
moment that seemed to last forever but could only have
been a second or two before she dragged her gaze away
to look down at the service sheet. But she couldn't read
any more, couldn't concentrate on anything but the
sudden revelation that this wasn't just attraction and
desire. This was love. The now and forever kind that up
to this point she'd only read or dreamed about, hoping
that one day it might happen to her, but with each
passing year having less expectation that she would be
one of the lucky ones. But, whatever happened now, life
would never be the same. If the voyage came to an end
and she never saw Thor again she might go on to find
happiness or sorrow, but she knew that life would never
be complete away from this one man with whom she had
fallen so desperately in love.

The service came to an end without her realising it.
Thor said, 'Amen.' Followed by, 'Tony, Zara, I want to
see you in my cabin.'

She stood there, still clutching the service sheet until
Mack came to take it from her. 'Don't worry, lass,' he
said, looking at her pale face. 'I'll have a word with the
skipper first.'

Zara couldn't speak, could only nod, not looking at him, and go over to the side, gripping the rail as she tried to control herself.

Tony came over to them and put his hand on her arm. 'You don't have to go, Zara. I'll tell him it was my fault.'

'Better both go when the skipper's ordered it,' Mack advised. He gave her a frowning look then led the way across the deck and down the companion-way. Thor's door was open. Mack gave a brief knock and went in, shutting the door behind him.

'Are you all right, Zara?' Tony asked. 'You don't look well.'

'No, I'm OK,' she said mechanically. She leaned against the wall, wishing she was anywhere but here with the prospect of having to face Thor. She wished she could be alone, with time to come to terms with this sudden upsurge of emotion, with this wonderful joy and fear that filled her heart.

But her face was still pale when Mack came out and Thor called them into his cabin. His shrewd glance went over them and his eyes frowned a little when he looked at Zara, but before he could speak Tony said, 'It's all my fault.'

Thor gave him a glance. 'I thought it might be. What happened?' But his eyes went back to Zara's lowered head.

'A blue towel had been left in the washing-machine by mistake and the uniforms came out a funny colour, so I asked Zara to get them white again for me.'

'I see.' Thor's frowning glance came back to Tony. 'It was done on purpose,' he said shortly. 'Someone thought it would be a good joke to put the towel in with the wash.'

'Really?' Tony looked both relieved and indignant. 'Of all the nerve! Who was it? I bet it was——' He broke off abruptly, not wanting to get anyone else in trouble.

He received a sardonic look from the skipper. 'Just pass on the message to the rest of the crew that if they must play practical jokes then they should at least have the decency not to let others put them right. It must have meant a lot of extra work for Zara to cover up for you. Now get going.'

'Aye, aye, Skipper.'

They turned to leave, but Thor said, 'Zara. Just a moment.'

She turned reluctantly back, her eyes going swiftly to his face and then down again. 'Yes, sir?'

Thor frowned. 'You look tired,' he said roughly. 'You shouldn't have stayed up so late. In future let Tony sort out his own problems.'

'It wasn't that. I—I didn't sleep very well.'

The skipper's face tightened. 'I hope I didn't embarrass you last night,' he said woodenly.

'Oh, no.' But Zara's cheeks were suffused with colour.

'I hope you weren't afraid that I'd discipline you for helping Tony. I try to be fair, Zara; I don't bawl out people who don't deserve it.'

Zara lifted her head at that and for the first time looked him directly in the face. 'Don't you?' she said on a dry note.

'You're thinking of when I wouldn't believe your story when you first came to see me.' He gave an impatient shrug. 'All right, I admit I was wrong about you. But if you look at it from my point of view you **must** realise that——'

'Yes, all right,' Zara broke in shortly. 'Can I go now?'

Her interruption had been ill-mannered, to say the least, and as Thor got slowly to his feet she expected him to tell her off again, but instead his voice was almost gentle as he said, 'Is there something the matter, Zara? Can I help in any way?'

She would rather he had bawled her out; his anger was easier to withstand than his gentleness. '*No*,' she said forcefully. Then, on a mirthless, painful laugh, 'There's nothing *you* can do. *Please*. Can I go now?'

He nodded, frowning, but said, 'Remember that I'm always here if you change your mind. And whatever you care to say to me will always be between just the two of us. No one else will ever know.'

Her eyes went to his face; she was wondering what he would think if she told him the truth, told him that he was the one man in the world she would ever love. Would he laugh at her? Or be angry or embarrassed? She would never know, because she could never tell him. Trying to hide her painfully new and raw feelings, Zara nodded and turned to leave.

This time he let her go, and Zara ran to shut herself in her own cabin, the only place where she could find any privacy on the ship. She sat on her bunk, her knees drawn up against her chest, her head in her hands, trying to be calm, trying to work things out, but filled at one moment with exultance and the next with despair. Most of the time she wished fervently that this hadn't happened, that it had just been sexual attraction. The game of love. A game that was amusing to play even with someone as enigmatic as Thor; even more so, perhaps, because he would have been more of a challenge. Zara could imagine herself using her feminine wiles to set out to attract him despite himself. Fun if she succeeded, and no great loss if she didn't. But now everything had changed and it could never be a game, only deadly serious. To be rejected by Thor would be unbearable, so it would be better not to try. But not to try, to let her chance for supreme happiness slip through her fingers from fear of failure, would be even more unbearable.

Her feelings riotous, Zara went about her work that day in a confused daze, but luckily, it being Sunday, she wasn't expected to do very much except make the lunchtime sandwiches and cook the evening meal. The crew made a special occasion of the traditional Sunday roast, putting on clean clothes and smartening themselves up. Zara supposed she'd better do the same and put on the sundress that Thor had given her. Her skin had tanned to a pale gold and luckily her eyelashes were naturally dark, in contrast to her fair hair, so that she had no need to apply any make-up, although tonight some blusher would have enhanced her pale cheeks.

Thor took a chair at the head of the long table and the crew all sat round on the benches. Tony helped Zara to bring in the vegetable dishes, but she carried the roast on its large plate and put it in front of Thor to carve. She didn't look at him as she did so but she knew that his eyes had run over her in the sundress. Was he thinking of the girl it had originally belonged to? Zara tried to put the torturing thoughts out of her mind as she took her place further down the table, next to Pete so that she could help him cut up his food.

Thor said grace and expertly attacked the meat so that they were soon served. Zara helped Pete but found that she had no appetite for her own food and was unable to join animatedly in conversation as she normally did.

'Aren't you hungry, Zara?'

She looked up as Thor spoke to her and tried to smile. Doing her best to keep her voice light, she said, 'Well, you know how it is; having to cook the food puts you off eating it.'

'It doesn't usually deter you,' Pete said with a grin. 'I'd say you have a very healthy appetite.'

'So have you when Zara's cooked it,' Mack pointed out. 'In fact, I'd say you eat like a pig.'

Glad of their usual good-natured ribaldry, Zara was able to sit back in unnoticed silence. When they'd finished the first course she cleared away the dishes and set a big steamed pudding and a large jug of custard on the table, then slipped back in the galley where she busied herself with loading the dishwasher. Mack called out, asking her if she wanted any. 'No thanks; too fattening,' she called back.

Slipping out of the galley in the other direction, Zara went up on deck. Arne was at the helm and Steve was part-way up the mast, keeping watch. The sun had gone down, and only a golden haze in the sky to the west was left of the day. A day I shall remember for the rest of my life, Zara thought as she went up to lean on the bow rail. She stood there for a while, letting her thoughts take their chaotic course, unable to think straight tonight. One moment she was full of hope, the next of despair so acute that tears came to her eyes.

Thor's step sounded behind her and her eyes were too full for her to completely blink back the tears before he said her name and she had to turn and face him. 'Yes?'

She was standing near the bow light and his eyes raked her face. 'The men want to thank you for that meal; they said it was the best Sunday meal they've ever had on board ship.'

'That was—kind of them. I'm glad they enjoyed it.'

'Are you feeling unwell, Zara?'

She shook her head and tried to look the picture of health. 'No, I'm fine, really.'

Thor nodded but was obviously unconvinced. 'You made a good job of altering that dress. It suits you.'

A poor compliment but the best he'd given her. Lifting her head, she said, 'Who did it belong to?'

His mouth thinned. 'A girl who came on a voyage with us once.'

'As passenger or crew?'

He gave a harsh laugh. 'Oh, definitely as a passenger.'

'Was she a girlfriend of one of the crew? Your girlfriend, perhaps?'

Thor's eyes came down to her face, so cold that they made her shiver as if someone had walked over her grave. 'Why so interested?'

She put her arms across her chest and gripped her shoulders. Her voice rising, she said, 'I'm not. I just wondered whose dress it was, that's all. It was just something to say. Excuse me.' And she ran to the companion-way and hurried below.

But Thor followed her down, jumping down the steps so that he was only a few paces behind her when she reached the corridor. It was empty, the crew still in the saloon. 'Zara, wait.'

She stood still with her back towards him, but he put a hand on her arm and turned her to face him. Her whole body trembled and she quickly drew away, her heart thumping. Thor frowned. He said, 'I'm sorry if I upset you. I didn't mean to.' She didn't answer, just stood staring up at him, her insides doing crazy things. 'Zara, are you afraid of me?' he asked abruptly.

For a long moment she didn't answer, but then, her vulnerable eyes still on his face, she said, 'Yes. Yes, I am afraid of you.'

'But you've no need to be.' He put his hands on her arms to emphasise his words. 'A ship's captain has to be strict. But I didn't mean to make you afraid; that's the last thing I want.'

His grip on her arms had tightened a little. Great aching waves of desire filled her at his nearness, at his touch. 'Is it?' Zara breathed, her lips parting sensuously.

'Why, yes. I——' Thor became abruptly silent as he gazed down at her and saw the dark desire in her face. Zara could feel the sudden tension in his hands. She waited, longed, hungered for him to kiss her. His fingers dug into her arms, hurting her, but she was oblivious to the pain. She lifted her own arms to put them on his chest, moved nearer to him. He took a gasping breath and then his mouth was on hers, his lips burning, passionate. Zara gave a moan of joy and returned his kiss with fierce hunger, her senses reeling. Happiness soared, peaked, as she put her arms around his neck and moved close against him, her body urgent with need. She heard Thor groan, deep in his throat, and his hands went to her waist. She murmured his name against his mouth, and was unaware of his sudden stillness. But then he pushed her violently from him, sending her staggering back against the wall. 'You little vixen!' He stared at her, his chest heaving, his hands clenched into white-knuckled fists. 'I was right about you all along!' he exclaimed savagely. With a look of withering revulsion he strode away, leaving Zara with her world in ashes around her.

CHAPTER SIX

IT WOULD have been easy to pretend to be ill and stay in her cabin the following day, but Zara had too much pride for that. She was up at the usual time, preparing breakfast for the crew, apparently as cheerful as ever. So cheerful, in fact, that no one noticed the dark shadows of a sleepless night around her eyes, or that her voice was so over-bright as to be on the edge of hysteria. But she got Ken to take Thor's breakfast along to his cabin; seeing him this morning was more than she could take. Pretending that nothing had happened in front of the crew was one thing; facing Thor was something else.

Luckily they were sailing through a busy sea-lane that morning so he was either in the navigation-room watching the radar screen, or else standing by the helmsman, so that she didn't run into him until the afternoon. Zara had gone up on deck to throw the scraps from lunch over the side. Unfortunately the ship tacked on to a new course just as she emptied the bucket overboard and several scraps of tomato and pieces of apple peel blew back on to the clean deck. Zara bent to pick them up and found Thor standing over her.

'Haven't you learnt something as simple as telling which way the wind is blowing yet?' he demanded harshly. 'Get rid of those and then clean that deck again.'

Zara gave him one swift look and immediately hurried to obey him, trying desperately to ignore the angry contempt in his eyes. When she'd cleaned the deck and gone below Steve came down after her.

'The skipper says you haven't cleared up properly and you're to do the deck again.' He gave her a puzzled glance. 'It looks all right to me.'

'I must have missed something,' Zara said lightly, and this time took a scrubbing brush and went down on her knees to do it again.

As she finished she became aware of Thor standing near by, watching her. He walked over to take a closer look, but even his cold eyes could find no further fault. 'All right, that will do,' he said grudgingly.

But at dinner that evening he had reason to complain because Zara had become lost in her own thoughts while she was cooking a pie and it looked more like one of Ken's offerings than her own usually succulent meals. And she'd forgotten to put the bread in the oven until almost the last minute, so that it wasn't cooked enough. Thor pointed out the mistakes to her, his voice heavy with sarcasm, while Zara looked stonily down at her plate. After the meal he came into the galley, went round it minutely and ordered her to clean it there and then. 'This place is filthy,' he said shortly. 'I'm surprised we haven't all gone down with stomach trouble. You don't go off duty until it's spotless.'

Once Zara would have fired up in indignation, knowing that she kept the place pristine compared with the way Ken had left it, but not today; today she had no fight left in her.

The men in the saloon had heard Thor, and heard his complaints, too, during dinner. His obvious anger had silenced their usual banter and it had been an uneasy meal. When Thor went back to his cabin Tony and Pete came into the galley. 'What's up with the skipper?' Pete wanted to know. 'He's like a bear with a sore head.'

Zara shrugged. 'I burnt the pie.'

'Yeah, but Ken used to burn everything and the skipper never went for him the way he went for you tonight. What have you done to upset him?'

'How should I know?' Zara said irritably. 'Look, I'd better make a start on cleaning out the galley or else he'll be having another go at me.'

'I'll give you a hand if you like,' Tony offered.

She managed to find a smile for him. 'Thanks, but there really isn't enough space for two people to work. Don't worry, I'll manage.'

Zara set grimly to work and scrubbed and cleaned until her hands were sore. When she'd finished the place shone, and she looked with weary pride at her handiwork, then went gratefully to bed. The work had one blessing—she fell immediately asleep, only to wake with a start as someone banged on her door and yelled at her to come out.

Still more than half asleep, Zara got out of bed, hair dishevelled, her silk nightdress clinging to her warm body. Pulling open the door, she said, 'What is it? Is the ship sinking?'

'No.' Thor's eyes swept over her and returned grimly to her face, his jaw hardening. 'Who gave you permission to go to bed before you'd finished the job I gave you?'

'But I cleaned the galley,' she protested.

'It might be clean by your standards but it isn't by mine. Get dressed and report back there in five minutes.'

Anger began to fill her soul as she stared at him, at his hard, inflexible features, but then a great ache of lonely wretchedness took its place and she turned to obey him. 'All right.'

'What did you say?' he demanded harshly.

'I said all right, I'll——' She paused, her eyes not meeting his. 'I mean, aye, aye, Skipper.'

'That's better.'

He had pulled pans out of cupboards, taken shelves out of the oven, moved the microwave, in order to find places she had missed. 'I said I wanted to find this galley spotless,' he reminded her curtly. 'Now get to it. I'll be round to check.'

It was gone two in the morning before he was satisfied and let her go to bed. The watch had changed at midnight, and the men coming into the galley for a nightcap had found her with a bucket of soapy water, scrubbing out behind the electric cooker. Steve immediately pulled her to her feet and took the brush from her. 'Here, let me do that.'

But Thor had come in behind him. 'It's the girl's job, let her get on with it.'

'But Zara's out on her feet, Skipper.'

'If ever you become the captain of a ship—which I very much doubt—then you'll be able to give your own orders; until then you'll obey mine. Now get your drinks and leave her to get on with it,' Thor snapped acidly.

'What the hell's got into the skipper?' Steve demanded of them all when he'd gone.

Nobody answered, and Zara avoided his eyes as she took the brush back. 'Thanks, anyway.'

When Thor came back he managed to find some dust on a piece of trunking near the ceiling that she couldn't even see. His eyes challenged her as he told her to clean it, but she didn't rise to the bait; she had no intention of giving him an excuse to tell her again what he thought of her, or the satisfaction of making her cry. She found a box to stand on and began to clean, her eyes so tired that she could hardly keep them open. The ship pitched as it met an unexpectedly high wave and Zara fell off the box, jarring her elbow against the sink. For a few minutes there were stars inside the ship as well as out. Then she took a deep breath and somehow managed to finish the job she'd been given with her left hand.

When he came back this time she was leaning against the wall, her arms folded so that one hand was under the bruised elbow, her mouth set into a hard, grim line of determination. She wouldn't cry, she wouldn't! Her eyes followed him malevolently as Thor went over every inch of the galley, but then he stood back, disappointed; the ovens and cupboards were pristine clean, even the bottoms of the pans so shiny that you could see your face in them. There was nothing he could find to complain about. 'All right, you can go—but just make sure the galley stays this way in future.'

She looked at him, her gaze wide and unblinking.

'I said you could go,' Thor repeated.

'Are you ordering me to?'

His mouth twisted sardonically. 'Not unless you want to stay and clean it again.'

She didn't answer and he gave her a grim smile before he walked away. When he'd gone Zara gave a deep, trembling sigh and unfolded her arms. Her hands were sore and cracked, and her elbow throbbed painfully. When she got to her cabin she had no strength left to take off her clothes, but lay down on the bunk and went straight into an exhausted sleep.

Thor's actions set a pattern for the following days. He found fault with everything she did and punished her unmercifully, making her do every job two or three times over. Zara knew instinctively why he was so angry with her—not just because he again believed her to be the cheap little tramp he'd thought her in the first place, but mostly because he hadn't been able to resist kissing her himself. And by doing so had he betrayed the woman he loved, the woman who wrote to him from Denmark? So he took his anger at his own weakness out on her, and did so with the heavy hand of revenge. When the men saw and heard they looked at him in astonishment, not recognising this aspect of him. When they went to help Zara they were curtly told to leave her alone, or were given extra work themselves to keep them busy. From being a happy, friendly ship, the atmosphere changed, grew tense. Zara accepted everything Thor threw at her stoically, making no complaint, determined not to let him break her. But there were no rubber gloves to protect soft hands on this originally all-male ship and they became very sore, her fingertips raw and bleeding. She managed to hide it most of the time but one day Mack came unexpectedly into the galley and found her trying to fasten plastic bags over her hands.

'What on earth are you doing?'

'Oh! Nothing.' Zara dropped the bags and put her hands behind her.

'Let me have a look.'

'It's nothing, really,' she said with a forced laugh. 'Just vanity.'

But he took hold of her arm and made her turn her hand over so that he could see. 'Good grief, Zara! Your fingers are raw. You must have them treated and bandaged at once. Come on, I'll——'

'*No.* No, they're all right.'

'Rubbish! They must hurt like hell. You must go along to the skipper and...' He broke off when he saw the alarm in her eyes. 'Zara, what is this between you and the skipper? He's been treating you like dirt for the last week. What have you done to make him so angry?'

'It doesn't matter.' She put a weary hand up to her forehead.

'Of course it matters. He can't go on treating you like this. I'm going to see him and talk some sense into him,' he said angrily.

He went to turn away but Zara caught hold of his arm. 'Mack, no, please. You'll only make things worse. He'll think I sent you.'

'But this can't go on. You can't take any more of this kind of treatment.'

'Yes, I can,' she answered fiercely. 'I can take as much as he hands out. I'm *not* going to let him get to me.'

Mack stared at her. 'This is between you and the skipper—is that what you're saying?'

'Yes, I suppose so.' She looked away, afraid of revealing too much.

But Mack must have drawn his own conclusions because he said shortly, 'Then it's about time you sorted it out. You can't go on like this.'

'There's less than a week of the voyage to go,' Zara reminded him. 'So things will sort themselves out then, won't they?'

He gave a derisive snort. 'I doubt it. But in the meantime you've got to have something done about those hands. No, don't worry; I'll go to the skipper's cabin and get the first-aid box and bind them up myself. If he says anything I'll tell him you've burnt your hands on the cooker.'

Zara opened her mouth to protest but shut it again when she saw the determination on his weathered face. He came back shortly with the first-aid box and shook his head to the anxious question in her eyes.

'It's all right; he wasn't there.' He bandaged her hands, but said, 'I'm not much good at this. The skipper's the expert; he's the only one with any medical knowledge on the ship.'

'They're fine. Thank you. Now if you'll just fasten those plastic bags over my hands I'll be able to get on with cleaning out the showers and the head.'

'You shouldn't be doing that,' he said disapprovingly.

'Someone has to do it. There are some elastic bands there to fasten the wrists.'

Mack did as she asked but looked dubiously at the result. 'They don't look as if they'll last long. I'll try and make you something better.'

'Thanks, Mack, you're a dear.' Reaching up, she gave him a peck on the cheek.

'Oh, yes, what's this, then?' Zara's heart plunged sickeningly but she gave a sigh of relief when she saw it was only Pete. 'Making out with the officers, I see.'

'Zara and I have a mutual-admiration society that doesn't include you lower ranks,' Mack told him loftily. 'How's your arm?' he added pointedly.

'Hurts like hell,' Pete lied cheerfully. 'Zara, why have you got bags on your hands?'

'It's the latest fashion.'

Pete sighed. 'Ask a silly question...' He went over to pour himself a mug of coffee. 'But seriously, though, why——?' He turned and became silent as Thor came into the galley.

The skipper's eyes immediately settled on the first-aid box still open on the table. 'Who's hurt?' he asked Mack.

'No one,' the mate answered blandly. 'Just checking on Pete's arm, that's all.'

Pete blinked but managed to keep his face straight as Thor nodded, then looked coldly at Zara, who had her arms behind her. 'I thought I told you to clean out the showers. Get on with it instead of wasting the crew's time.'

He went to get himself a coffee and Zara picked up her bucket and slipped out while his back was turned. She went to the showers and began to clean them with the washing-soda solution in the bucket. She had come to know that bucket really well; it had become her constant companion in the last week. When I get off this ship, she thought, I am going to take the bucket and this rotten scrubbing brush and ceremoniously burn them. But at least Mack's bandages and the plastic bags were saving her hands from the burning washing-soda, which was a wonderful relief.

The rest of that day was almost bearable, especially as Thor ate his meals in his own cabin, but the next evening things came suddenly to a head. Thor chose to eat in the saloon, so Zara took the bandages off her hands so that he wouldn't notice. She had cooked a casserole for dinner; the men had had their starter and were waiting for her to serve it, but as Zara took the dish from the oven the heat went through the oven cloth she was using and seared her fingers with excruciating pain. She gave an involuntary cry and the casserole dish slipped from her hands. Instinctively she tried to save it, but the lid came off and sent hot stew over her right hand. She screamed and the men came rushing in.

Zara was leaning against the work units, gasping with pain. They all went to help her but Thor yelled out, 'Keep back, there's no room for all of you.' He glared at Zara. 'Find us something else to eat and then clear up the mess.'

'But she's scalded herself!' Steve exclaimed.

'Then it will teach her not to be so damn clumsy in future.' Thor went to turn to go back into the saloon but found his way barred by the men, who were staring at him with stunned, angry expressions on their faces.

Then Mack shouldered his way through. He was physically much less of a man than Thor but he faced up to him squarely. 'Why the hell don't you pick on someone your own size, Skipper?' he demanded. 'Or is a helpless girl your idea of a fair opponent?' Suddenly he whirled and grabbed Zara's arm, pulling her forward.

'No!' She tried to resist but he took hold of her wrists and thrust her hands, palm upwards, under Thor's eyes.

'Look at her hands. She's not a man; she's not hardened to the kind of work you've been making her do. But you've been picking on her, victimising her. I don't know what your reasons are, and I don't care. But it's gone far enough.'

Thor was listening to him but his eyes were fixed on Zara's hands. She tried to pull out of Mack's grip, angry with him for betraying her. 'I'm all right.'

'You're not all right. Your hands need bandaging again and now you've scalded them. Steve, go and get the first-aid box,' Mack ordered.

Steve ran to obey him while Zara stuck her hand under the tap. Thor lifted his head and looked round at the men in the doorway and then at Mack. His face seemed strangely pale and drawn.

'Here it is.' Steve came hurrying back.

Mack drew her into the saloon. 'Come and sit down, Zara, and let me have a look. Steve, find the ointment for burns.'

But Thor put out an arm to stop him. 'No, I'll do it. Ken, perhaps you could rustle up something to eat? The rest of you can clean up the galley.'

The men looked at each other, but their moment of near-rebellion was over and they went to obey him. After a moment's hesitation Mack moved out of the way and let Thor take over, but he stood beside them, watching.

'You should have had these treated before,' Thor said shortly as he took hold of her hands to examine them.

'She did, but she took the bandages off so you wouldn't notice,' Mack said curtly. 'She's proud and stubborn as a mule. If you ask me you're as mad as each other.'

'I didn't ask you,' Thor said shortly. 'Why don't you go on deck and take over the ship?'

Mack's hesitation was longer this time, but at length he said to Zara, 'Send someone for me if you need me.'

She nodded, not looking at him, concentrating hard on not letting her hands tremble in Thor's grip.

When Mack had gone Thor said roughly, 'You little fool. Why didn't you tell me?'

His harsh tone and being called a fool helped, strangely enough. Zara's hands steadied and her grey eyes, cool and clear, settled on his bent head. 'You know why,' she answered shortly.

Briefly his eyes came up to meet hers. There was anger in them, but as he looked at her face they became frowning, puzzled. 'I don't understand you,' he said shortly. 'One moment you behave like a cheap little tart, but then you——' he glanced down at her poor hands '—then you're proud and obstinate enough to go as far as this.'

'Even cheap little tarts can have their pride,' Zara said mockingly.

'If they had pride they wouldn't be tarts in the first place.' Thor frowned again, realising what he'd said. 'You don't add up.'

Still flippant, she said, 'Maybe you're just bad at arithmetic.'

Ken came in then, carrying a basket of rolls. 'We've managed to save most of the casserole,' he said cheerfully. 'And the spuds and bread are OK, so we can eat as soon as you've finished, Skipper.'

'Good.' Thor immediately became brisk again, quickly finishing bandaging her hands. 'There, that should do for now. The scald isn't too bad. You'd better keep them out of water, though. I'll take another look at them tomorrow.'

'Thank you,' Zara said automatically.

But he thought she was still being sarcastic and said harshly, 'All right; you don't have to rub it in.'

'I wasn't. I . . .' But he had already turned away.

It was an uneasy truce. Now she was relieved of the heaviest duties Zara's hands soon began to heal, but she wasn't sure whether she wanted them to or not, because every morning, after breakfast, she had to go along to Thor's cabin to have them dressed. It was a half-hour she both looked forward to and yet dreaded. It gave her a little time to be close to him, to feel his touch, to let the love in her heart grow and be warmed by his nearness. But Thor's manner was always rigidly cold and brisk, his hands efficient as he applied salve and dressings. There was no gentleness in his touch, no sign that he had ever felt anything for her other than cool contempt. He found nothing to say to her beyond what was necessary—an injunction to remove the bandages at night or to tell her off if they got wet.

'I had to wash myself,' she protested.

He merely nodded, as if he wasn't really interested, but later that day Mack brought along a pair of gloves fashioned out of somebody's bright red oilskin.

'Oh, Mack, they're just what I need. Thanks a lot. But you didn't cut up your own wet-weather gear to make them, did you?'

Mack shook his head. 'The skipper gave me his spare jacket.'

'Oh.' Zara could find nothing more to say to that, but not being able to do much work gave her plenty of time to think. She spent most of her time sunbathing out on the deck. She had a book in her hands but the pages only got turned when she remembered to do so, and she wore sunglasses so that no one would notice if her glance went often to where Thor stood beside the helmsman. Her thoughts seemed always to be full of him, as if there were nothing else in the world worth thinking about any more. Being in love had changed her whole life, her feelings, her thoughts, her ambitions, her dreams; nothing was the same. Even the happy optimism which had carried her through, despite all the bad things that had happened to her over the years, had now deserted her. She felt vulnerable and low, convinced that she would never find happiness with Thor. Trust her to fall in love with a woman-hater.

Although he no longer picked on her and he showed no outward antagonism, there was still this wall of cold reserve that Zara couldn't break through. In fact, she didn't even try. It was as if love had sapped all her energy, all her self-confidence and natural resilience. She felt punch-drunk and bemused. Even her love of life had taken a nasty jolt: it stretched long and empty before her.

As the days passed the hours that were left became both more painful and more precious. Thor made no secret of the fact that he would put her ashore the minute they got to Rhodes, and would be glad to see her go. In some ways Zara wanted to get there too, so that she wouldn't have the pain of seeing him every day, so that she could try to get over these stupid, soul-destroying emotions alone and with some kind of dignity. But the thought of never in her life seeing him again was almost unbearable, and in those moments she longed for time to slow, to stop, so that she could at least rest her eyes on Thor's tall, muscular figure and think of what might have been.

'I didn't know you were from down under as well, Zara,' Pete commented as he lay stretched out beside her.

Zara blinked and came back to her surroundings. 'What do you mean?'

Leaning forward, he took hold of her book and turned it. 'You've been reading upside down for the last half an hour.'

'Oh.' She flushed. 'I—er—must have fallen asleep,' she said feebly.

'Well, you were certainly daydreaming. Want me to rub some oil on your shoulders?'

'Please.'

Zara had on her home-made bikini and her skin was tanning to a beautiful deep gold, but the Mediterranean sun was becoming stronger with every mile they sailed and it was as well to be careful. With only one good hand between them it wasn't easy, and Pete's efforts made them both laugh. Thor was further along the deck, teaching Steve how to plot their position using the old-fashioned sextant. Their laughter distracted him and he glanced across. For a moment he became very still and tense, totally abstracted, his eyes fixed on them, but then Thor turned abruptly back to Steve.

'Pity you can't do my back for me,' Pete commented wistfully.

'You don't need it; your skin is as thick as rhinoceros hide already.'

'Oh, thanks.' But Pete was used to being teased and rather liked it. Settling back, he said, 'What are you going to do when you get to Rhodes, Zara?'

'I wish I knew. Hopefully my replacement credit card will have arrived and I'll be able to draw some money out of my account. I don't think I'll have enough for my fare back to England, though, so I'll probably have to look for work in Rhodes. I might even be lucky enough to get a job as an entertainer on a cruise liner or at a hotel somewhere on the island.'

'Why don't you come over to Oz?'

'Australia? I wouldn't want to go that far alone. And, besides, I don't have enough money.'

'You could come with me,' Pete surprised her by saying.

'But you don't have to leave the ship. Thor—the skipper will let you stay on even if your arm is broken, won't he?'

'Sure, but I don't intend to stay on it forever. I joined the crew so that I'd see something of Europe and the old country, but I've got a job waiting for me on my dad's station back in Oz.'

'You mean you're going to work for the railway?'

Pete gave a guffaw of laughter. 'No, idiot. It's a sheep station in the outback. You'd like it there.'

'But would it like me?' Zara said with a smile. 'Do sheep and showgirls mix?'

'I reckon you'd get along anywhere you went. You've got guts, Zara.'

Coming from Pete, that was quite a compliment. Her voice husky, Zara leant forward and touched his bare shoulder gratefully. 'Thanks, Pete, but I——' A shadow fell across them and Zara glanced up. Thor and Steve had moved further down the deck and had come within earshot. She stood up in one lithe, graceful movement. 'Excuse me, I think I'd better go and make sure Ken doesn't burn the dinner.'

Thor watched her go, a sardonic curve to his mouth, and she could guess exactly what he was thinking: that she was trying her wiles on Pete now. Bitterly she thought that, no matter what she did, she just couldn't win.

With Zara standing over him Ken's cooking had improved tremendously, but if she wasn't there to remind him he would get bored and listen to the radio or pick up a magazine while he waited for things to cook, so that he forgot them and they burnt again. Zara tried to instil into him some interest and pride in what he was doing, but the poor man just wasn't domestically minded and hated every minute he had to spend in the galley. Almost any other member of the crew would have done better, Zara thought with a sigh, but Ken was the one who could most be spared when the wind was blowing and they didn't need the engines.

It was almost exactly three weeks since Zara had stowed away on the ship when they sailed into Rhodes harbour. They did so in the morning, approaching the island from the west so that the full strength of the sun lit their sails, turning them to bright gold. Thor had ordered the flags of every nationality on board to be flown as well as the Union Jack, so that the *Spirit of the Wind* looked a brave and beautiful sight as she neared the island. They rounded the headland, so close to shore that Zara could see people watching and waving to them.

And then they were in sight of the immense range of walls and towers and turreted gateways of the fortress of the Knights of St John of Jerusalem that dominated the harbour.

Zara stood on deck, entranced by what she saw, but trying to keep out of the way of the crew as they furled the sails and Thor brought his ship into the ancient port of Mandraki, through an entrance so narrow that the legendary Colossus of Rhodes was supposed to have straddled it. Now only an ancient fort and a row of windmills lined the harbour bar, but they were picturesque enough for most of the crew who had their cameras out, snapping the scene.

They moored efficiently alongside the dock and immediately attracted a crowd of people who came to look and admire, their eyes nostalgic and envious. The gangplank went down and the harbour-master came on board together with a Customs officer. Zara saw them and the uplift she'd got from seeing the lovely harbour sank at once. Thor took the officials down below to his cabin and she could guess that one of his first requests was that she should be put ashore.

Seeing her dejected face, Tony came over to her and gave her a clumsy pat on the shoulder. 'Don't worry, Zara. After all, you'll soon be home now.'

'Home?' She gave a bitter little laugh. 'I don't have a real home. I've got nowhere to go and nowhere I want to go.'

'We don't want to lose you, either,' Tony said sympathetically. 'Do we, fellas?'

'What's that?' Ken, Arne and Steve wandered over.

'I was just saying that we don't want to lose Zara.'

'That we don't,' Ken said forcefully. 'I'll have to do all the cooking again now.'

'And we've got to eat it,' Arne said with a groan. 'Why don't you ask the skipper if you can stay on as regular crew while we're in Rhodes? That way you'll earn some money and you'll be among friends.'

'I'd love to,' Zara said wistfully. 'But it's no good; you know he wants to get rid of me. My bag's all packed and I'm ready to go.'

'It's a shame,' Tony said heatedly. 'We really need Zara, and yet the skipper's going to put her ashore not knowing where she's going to stay or even if she's got any money to pay for her lodging, let alone a flight back to England.'

'He let me stay on board,' Zara pointed out quickly. 'That's all he promised. I always knew I'd have to leave the ship here.'

Arne nodded. 'That's so.'

The men moved away to where Mack and Pete were standing, and they began to talk together. Presently Thor and the officials came on deck and Thor strode over to Pete. 'I've arranged for you to go to the local hospital straight away to have your arm X-rayed. Here's the address and some Greek money for a taxi. If it's found to be broken and you're likely to be a long time, then phone the harbour-master's office and they'll give us the message.'

Pete took the money. 'Right oh, Skipper. Thanks. I'll—er—go and change my clothes first.'

Thor nodded and turned to Zara. 'Could you come to my cabin, please?'

Trying not to show any emotion, Zara followed him as he turned away.

'I've spoken to the Customs about you,' he said abruptly. 'Your replacement passport hasn't been sent to them. I'll have to get on to the British consul in the town and find out what's happening. But this letter arrived from your bank.' He handed it to her and Zara took it without opening it. 'I've explained the position to the authorities here and they've said that as soon as you get your passport you'll be allowed to leave Rhodes. Unfortunately, until it arrives you'll have to stay on the ship. But with any luck I should be able to pick it up for you later today so that you can go ashore.' He nodded dismissively. 'All right, you can go.'

If anything, Thor's voice was even more hard and unrelenting than usual. He scarcely looked at her as he spoke and there was a terse brusqueness in his manner that was little short of outright rudeness. Zara didn't deserve that from him. It wasn't her fault that he had for a brief moment succumbed to his own weakness, his own desires. Head high, she said clearly, 'I should like to thank you for not taking me back to Oran. I'm very grateful that you let me stay on board. I'm—I'm ready to leave as soon as you wish.'

He raised his head at that, and for a moment the mask was down and she saw torment in his eyes. But then he looked away and only his tightened knuckles betrayed his inner tension. He nodded curtly. 'I'll let you know when your passport arrives.'

Zara came out of his cabin feeling slightly unsteady. Going into the saloon, she sat down and looked at the envelope but found that her hands were shaking too much to hold it. That one glance had revealed so much. She had thought Thor's actions against her to be motivated by anger, but maybe there was more than that. Maybe he did feel something for her and was trying to fight it. Perhaps it was because he wanted her that he was so desperate to get rid of her and put temptation miles away. The thought took her breath away, and for a moment her heart filled with hope. If he cared for her, if he wanted her, then maybe there was still a chance.

But the next moment her hopes plunged. Even if Thor did feel something for her he had made it very evident that he wasn't going to surrender to it. Whatever his reasons were, he was determined that he wanted nothing to do with her. There was no alternative but to leave and try to forget him. She gazed blankly into space for a while, feeling wretched, until Pete came looking for her.

'Zara?'

She blinked and looked round at him. 'Yes?'

'I'm going ashore to the hospital now. What happened with the skipper? Are you going ashore, too? I didn't want to miss saying goodbye to you.'

Zara shook her head. 'My passport hasn't come yet. The skipper said he would try to collect it this afternoon. Then I'll—then I'll leave.'

'Do you want to go?'

She looked down at the table and picked up the envelope, holding it so tightly that it creased. 'It's best I go; the skipper doesn't like women on board.'

'Is that letter from your mother?' Pete asked.

'This? No, it's from my bank.' She slit it open and read the enclosed letter, stared at it for a moment, then gave a hysterical, disbelieving laugh. 'That's all I need.'

'What is it?' Before she could stop him Pete reached forward and took the letter from her. 'It says your account is overdrawn and would you please make up the deficit. That all the money was drawn out in Oran.'

Zara laughed again, her tone bitter. 'Ali Messaad's idea of getting even with me for not falling into his arms, I suppose.'

'Well, that settles it,' Pete muttered half to himself. 'You can't leave the ship if you don't have any money.'

'Of course I can.' Zara took the letter back from him. 'I'm a British citizen; I can go to the consul and borrow some money until I get a job. No problem.' Pete opened his mouth and she said quickly, 'And don't go getting any ideas about offering to lend me some yourself, Pete, because I won't accept. You're a friend and I don't borrow from friends.' He opened his mouth again. 'And don't even think about telling the skipper. He offered me a working passage and that's what I've had. He doesn't owe me anything or I him, and that's the way I want it to stay.' She gave him an urgent look. 'Promise me you won't, Pete.'

He stood up, his face indignant. 'Can I get a word in now? OK, if you want to make a go of it on your own, that's your affair. But just let me know where you'll be staying, that's all. Will you promise to do that? We've been good mates and I'd like to keep in touch.'

She gave him a warm smile. 'Of course I will. Hope you get on all right at the hospital.'

He gave her a wink. 'I've an idea it will turn out to be just a sprain.'

When Zara went up on deck she found that Thor had gone ashore to meet the producer of the film in which the ship was to take part. Some of the men had gone ashore, too, glad to stretch their legs after the long voyage. Zara was a little hurt, thinking that she wouldn't be able to say goodbye to them, but she managed to be her bright, friendly self as she prepared the men's lunch.

'I've written out a list of the fresh stores you'll need,' she told Mack.

He was busy, supervising the filling of their fuel tanks from a tanker lorry on the dock, and merely gave her a nod and thrust the list in his pocket. Feeling in the way, Zara went back to the galley to make sure it was sparkling clean; she didn't want Thor to have a chance to criticise her even after she'd gone. Her hands were better now, she just wore a couple of waterproof band-aids on her right hand. The sound of a motor horn attracted her to the porthole and Zara looked out to see Pete arrive in a taxi, his arm out of the sling and a big grin on his face. Lifting his right arm, he turned to wave back down the dock, and she saw the other men strolling towards the ship. Pete waited for them and she grinned to herself as she imagined the comments he was getting from the other men. They stood laughing together for a few minutes, exchanging derisive remarks with the men leaning over the rail of the ship, but then Zara saw them look round and become silent as another taxi drew up and Thor got out. Her face tightening, she went up on deck to receive her passport.

The men had all come aboard and were standing around as if they were waiting for something. The tanker lorry had gone and the dock workers were still enjoying their lunchtime siesta. The sun beat down on the deck, and the day was hot, still, and momentarily quiet.

Thor turned when he saw Zara come on deck. 'Come down to my cabin, will you?'

But Mack stepped forward and said, 'Just a moment, Skipper. I think we'd all like to know what's happening to Zara.'

'It's her business.'

'Ours too, as shipmates.'

His eyes narrowing as they swept over the men, Thor said, 'Zara? It's up to you.'

Puzzled, she said, 'I don't mind their knowing. Of course not.'

'Very well.' Thor shrugged. 'The embassy in Athens wants one or two more details before they can issue you with a new passport.' Zara's hopes rose a little at this but were quickly dashed when he went on, 'However, I've persuaded the authorities to grant you temporary papers so that you can go ashore straight away. You won't, though, be allowed to leave Rhodes until your passport arrives, and you have to report to them once a day. Do you understand?'

'Yes, th-thank you.' Zara blinked, finding it suddenly hard to see.

'I appreciate the work you've done,' Thor added surprisingly. 'And I want you to take the wages you would have earned if you'd been a bona fide member of the crew.' He held some Greek money out to her, but Zara could only look at it, not knowing whether she could swallow her pride enough to take it.

'Just a minute, Skipper.' Mack stepped forward. 'We still need a cook; why not keep Zara on as regular crew?'

There was a murmur of agreement from the men, but Thor said shortly, 'I intend to hire a new cook while we're here.'

'Why take on someone new when we know that Zara's good? She makes the best steamed puddings this side of the Equator.'

'I've already told you I——'

'Fact is, Skipper,' Mack broke in, 'the men don't want anyone else.'

Thor's eyes narrowed. 'What are you saying?'

'Well, we had a bit of a chat and we decided we want Zara to stay. If you insist on her going... Well, there won't be any good grub on board so we thought we'd go ashore for a few weeks.'

'I don't have to remind you that your contracts cover the making of this film.'

'And you undertook to give us decent food.'

Zara stood, turned to stone, as the men faced each other. In one way it was the most overwhelming moment of her life; no one had ever supported her like this before and now all the men stood determinedly in front of Thor, putting their own jobs in jeopardy for her. But what good would it do? Even if he kept her on he would hate her all the more for it and there would be a bad atmosphere between Thor and the men.

She made a small movement of protest, but Mack held up his hand to stop her, and said persuasively, 'It would only be until the film is over, Skipper. We can't work unless we get decent grub.'

Cold blue eyes went over them, one by one. A few faces blanched but they all met his eyes squarely. Knowing when he was beaten, Thor said curtly, 'Very well. She stays until the film is over.'

'Thanks, Skipper.' Mack gave Zara a broad grin as Thor turned away.

She stared at him, her eyes full of gratitude, unable to speak. But then Thor called her name and she went over to him as he stood at the head of the companionway. He held out the money he had been going to give her.

'Your wages.' She hesitated, but he thrust it at her. 'Take it.' Slowly she reached out and did so, her eyes coming up to meet his. In a voice of savage anger, he said, 'Am I *never* to be rid of you?'

CHAPTER SEVEN

'ZARA? What did he say to you?'

She turned from staring after Thor to find the rest of the crew watching her. Taking a deep breath, she somehow managed to pull herself together and give them a pale-faced smile. 'It was so kind of you all to want me to stay. But you shouldn't have given Thor an ulti- matum like that; he'll be angry with you and——'

'No, he won't,' Mack corrected her. 'And we merely made a suggestion. Thing is, we've got used to your being around.'

'I'm very grateful.' But she gave an anxious frown.

'We're only thinking of our stomachs, Zara,' Pete told her with a grin.

'Is that how I reached your hearts?' She made the riposte with a smile but it quickly faded as the men dis- persed. Zara walked over to the rail and gripped it, her knuckles white.

'What's the matter, Zara?' Mack came over to her.

'Mack, it was wonderful of you all to stick up for me like that, but I ought to go. He—the skipper doesn't want me on board.'

'Lassie, you've got no money and no place to go. You've no room for pride.'

'I'd manage.' But being allowed to stay on the ship was a tremendous relief from every angle—except that of her personal feelings for Thor, of course. Going down to her cabin, Zara unpacked her few possessions and sat on the bunk to count the money Thor had given her.

He had been generous, there was enough to last her for
a couple of weeks at a hotel ashore—longer if she'd
found a cheap room to rent. She wondered if he'd heard
that her money had all been stolen; she'd asked Pete not
to tell Thor, but Mack obviously knew, so presumably
the rest of the crew did, too. Zara sighed, wondering
whether it might not be better to leave anyway. It would
definitely be wiser, but she knew she wouldn't, not while
there was a chance to still be near Thor.

As it turned out, she hardly saw him for the next
couple of days. Carpenters, painters, and a set designer
from the film unit came aboard and more or less took
over the ship, transforming its outward appearance into
that of a Turkish warship of the sixteenth century. Thor
was on deck the whole day, making sure they didn't
damage anything vital—like lowering the height of the
masts, as the set designer wanted at one point. At the
same time he was making sure that the ship had enough
provisions to feed both the crew and any film workers,
should it be necessary. It seemed that all the crew were
to be signed on by the film company as extras for one
month and would receive the current rate of pay on top
of their wages from the ship's owners. Zara hadn't
expected to be included, but the clerk from the film
company signed her on along with the others, and when
the women from the wardrobe department came on the
ship she was told to hide her hair under a turban, her
breasts under a baggy shirt, and take the part of the
ship's boy.

It was all new and exciting. Zara was kept as busy as
the rest of the crew, going to the market to buy fresh
fruit and vegetables, restocking the larder and the freezer,
and finding out how to cook the local produce, some of
which was entirely strange to her. It all helped a great
deal to take her mind off her problems. Work, the uni-

versal panacea for all ills, she thought wryly. There was little time in those first few hectic days to explore the island, but she did find time to write to her mother, telling her she'd got a job on a film, which should make her happy.

When the ship was ready they had to take the *Spirit* out to sea so that a film crew could take some long shots of her from cameras set up in a modern motor boat. They were also required to put on their costumes so that they'd get used to wearing them and handling the ship with them on. Most of the crew were bare to the waist above their baggy trousers, but Thor had been given grander officer's clothes and wore a full-length sort of coat with splits up the sides over his silk shirt and trousers. There was a wicked-looking scimitar strapped round his waist, and on his head he wore a very full white turban. He was greeted by laughter and derisive wolf-whistles by the men, but Zara thought he looked magnificent. Her heart, in its usual rebellious fashion, gave a great lurch when she saw him, and she had to turn away to hide the flare of longing in her eyes.

After only a few days in Rhodes it felt good to be back at sea again, to hear the slap of the waves and crack of the sails instead of the throb of traffic and clamour of a city. Zara got her sea-legs quickly this time and was able to run and help pull on ropes as the ship altered course at the direction of the film crew, who transmitted their orders to Thor via a radio attached to his belt. There was a lot of laughter as the men tried to get used to their turbans and baggy trousers, but Thor wore his as if he'd been born to them, and the thought of being his captive in ancient times sent a delicious shiver of excitement running along Zara's spine.

At lunchtime they took a break and Thor dropped anchor off a quiet bay on the east coast of the island. The motor boat with the film crew pulled alongside, and they came aboard, glad to stretch their legs. Zara went down below to prepare a snack but paused in the saloon to take off the turban. As she lifted it her hair cascaded down, like a tumbling mass of molten gold. She heard a sound behind her and swung round, her hair swirling. It was Thor. He had taken off his own turban and the coat and stood in the doorway in the silk shirt open to the waist. Caught by surprise, he had no time to hide the flame of desire in his eyes. For a few seconds that flame burnt into her, devoured her in fierce hunger, but then he dragged his gaze away with a sigh so deep that it was almost a groan, and walked quickly away.

That moment, so unexpected and so revealing, shook Zara. First it brought joy and a kind of giddy excitement to know that he still wanted her, and with it came a rebirth of optimism. If he felt that deeply, if he wanted her that much... Love and its rejection had devastated her, but now Zara felt the first seeds of hope. Perhaps, just possibly, there was still a chance. If she set out to attract him who knew what might come of it? After all, what had she to lose? Thor couldn't despise her more than he already did. And maybe his hurry to get rid of her hadn't been entirely contempt; maybe it had been because he didn't entirely trust himself with her around.

As she prepared the salad and bread Zara began to sing to herself, the first time she'd done so for weeks.

One of the film crew put his head round the door. 'Excuse me, I'm trying to find some ice.'

Renewed optimism made her give him a smile he didn't deserve. 'Here's the bucket. The ice is in the fridge. Help yourself.'

'Thanks.' He went over and opened the door. 'That's a nice voice you've got.' His eyes swept over her. 'You don't look like a galley slave.'

'I'm not. I'm a dancer by profession.'

'Yeah? How'd you come to be working on this ship? Are you married to one of the crew?'

'No. It's a long story.' Zara turned to take plates from a cupboard.

'So how come? Are you the captain's girl?'

He said it so casually, as if it meant so little. Zara straightened up, trying not to betray any emotion. Turning to face him, she said, 'No, I'm——' then stopped as she saw that Thor had come back and was standing behind him. 'I'm just an orphan of the storm,' she finished. 'I was stranded in Oran and the skipper was kind enough to let me work my passage.'

The man, unaware of Thor, leered at her. 'Yeah? A good-looking girl like you—I bet you worked it in his bed. Or was the deal with the whole of the crew?'

'If you've got what you want why don't you get yourself and your foul insinuations out of here?' Thor said curtly, making the man jump and leave hastily, the ice-bucket clutched in his arms.

'I'm sorry,' Thor said in the same curt tone. 'If he's rude to you again, let me know.'

'Yes, thanks.' She held his eyes. 'Is that why you didn't want me to stay on—because people might get that idea?'

He paused for a moment, and she could see a pulse beating at his temple, then he said, '*No*, that wasn't the reason.'

'I—I'm glad.' She looked away.

'Do you——?' Thor hesitated. 'Perhaps I shouldn't ask, but do you often get things like that said to you?'

'Quite often,' Zara admitted. 'Men think that because you're in show business you're easy and they can say what they like to you. They think that you must be broad-minded, so they tell you dirty jokes, and they think they have the right to touch you all the time; put their arm round you and—and handle you.' Her voice had un-knowingly grown bitter with remembrance and her knuckles tightened on the plate she held. But then Zara blinked and lifted her head. 'What—what did you come for?'

'What? Oh—to tell you not to prepare a meal for this evening. I've just had a message over the radio; the crew have been invited to a party to meet the film director and producer.'

She nodded. 'OK, Skipper.'

Thor paused, then said roughly, 'You're crew, so you go along, too.'

Her face lit. 'Thanks.'

The delight lasted all of two minutes. When he'd gone Zara realised that the age-old complaint of every woman was perfectly justified in this case; she hadn't got a thing to wear. But she did have the money that Thor had given her, and the shops in Rhodes stayed open very late.

As soon as they moored Zara ran down the gangplank and into the town. There were beautiful shops with gorgeous clothes in the new town, stores where wealthy tourists could buy the latest French and Italian fashions. She saw clothes that she knew would have looked great on her but were all far too expensive. Acutely aware of the passing time, Zara stopped a very chic-looking girl and asked her where to get good, cheap clothes. She was directed to a shop in a back street where she found ex-actly what she was looking for, a simple but well-cut sheath dress in a pale coral colour that fitted quite tightly to the hips and then belled out into a full skirt. A dress that managed to be sexy and feminine at the same time. Zara had just enough time and money left to buy a matching pair of strap sandals before she hurried back to the ship to wash her hair and get ready.

The men had tossed up to see which two would stay aboard the ship, and Steve and Arne had been the unlucky ones. 'I'll send Tony and Pete along to relieve you in two hours,' Thor was promising as Zara came up on deck behind him.

'Wow!' Pete gave a long whistle of appreciation as he saw her. 'You look a million dollars.'

The other men swung round immediately but Thor turned more slowly, almost reluctantly, his body stiff.

'You look great, Zara,' came from Tony.

And, 'You'll do us proud, lassie,' from Mack.

The others, too, added their compliments, but Thor had nothing to say. Yet his eyes were on her, taking in the new, sophisticated way she'd done her hair, the make-up that had skilfully underlined her best features without being overstated, her slim but curved figure in the coral dress, and the soft, suntanned bare skin of her shoulders and arms.

'You all look pretty good, too,' Zara returned with a smile.

The crew had smartened themselves up, putting on their best clothes, and Mack and Thor wore their dress uniforms of white jackets and trousers, epaulettes on the shoulders, their brass buttons shining. Mack looked very smart, but Thor's height made him look terrific. Zara couldn't decide whether she preferred him in his uniform or in his costume for the film.

'Ready to go, Skipper?' Mack asked when Thor still didn't speak.

'Yes, of course. I've ordered a couple of taxis,' he said unnecessarily, because they could all see them waiting on the dockside.

There was great competition to help Zara down the gangplank in her high heels and to sit in the taxi with her. In the end she went with Tony and Pete and Ken while the two officers shared the other cab. The party was being held in a hotel that the film company had more or less taken over, in the very north of the town on a headland that was also the most northerly point of the whole island.

The taxi Zara was in arrived first, but as ordinary crew members they stood in the entrance, waiting for Thor and Mack to arrive and lead the way in. When Thor got out of the taxi he glanced at Zara and hesitated for a moment as if he might offer her his arm, but then strode ahead with Mack following.

Their hosts came forward to meet them and Thor took care to introduce each of them by name. These high-flyers of the film world shook each of the crew by hand but were really only interested in Thor, and Mack to a lesser extent, and took them off to meet the stars of the film. 'Help yourselves to whatever you want,' the director's assistant said expansively to the rest of them.

It was a big party in the ballroom of the hotel. As they collected a drink from the bar and wandered around it became plain that a lot of locals had also been invited.

'I thought the party was just for us,' Tony remarked.

'Thought the leading lady was going to fall for your charms, did you?' Pete teased. He caught hold of Zara's hand. 'Come on, let's dance. We've only got two hours before we have to go back to the ship.'

'Hey, I ought to dance with Zara first,' Tony objected. 'I was the one who smuggled her on board.'

But Pete had already pulled her on to the dance-floor and begun an energetic if graceless jive.

'Who was your last partner—a kangaroo?' Zara exclaimed, hastily moving her foot out of the way of his for the second time.

Pete had soon used up enough energy to want another drink, and she danced with Tony and Ken in turn. Mack came over while she was dancing with Ken and claimed her for the next dance. 'As long as it's a slow one. I'm too old for all that jigging about.'

It was, and they danced sedately round, giving Zara a chance to look over Mack's shoulder and see that Thor was standing in a group of people in the far corner, an area tacitly set apart for the stars and the chief executives of the film company, plus a few people obviously thought important enough to join them.

Following her eyes, Mack said, 'He doesn't look out of place there, does he?'

'Who?' Zara prevaricated. 'Oh, you mean the skipper. No, I suppose not. I was looking at the celebrities. There must be quite a few big stars in the film; I recognise several people.' She turned to give Mack her whole attention. 'Do you—or rather the ship—take part in many films?'

'Quite a few, but we've been in a couple of television serials and a lot of commercials, too. You should ask Thor; he'd be able to tell you more about it.'

'I'm looking forward to when the actual filming starts,' she said with enthusiasm.

'I'm not; the film company take over the ship as if they own it.'

'Well, I suppose they do if they're hiring it. Don't be so——'

'Zara?'

She turned in surprise as a woman dancing by stopped and said her name. 'Tina! Hi, how are you? What are you doing here?'

'I'm working on the film. I'm the third belly-dancer on the left. But, if you're on the film too, how come I haven't seen you around? I thought I knew all the dancers.'

'No, I'm not—at least, not as a dancer.' Zara laughed. 'We're causing a traffic jam. See you at the bar after this dance.'

'A friend?' Mack queried.

'We were in the same chorus line some years ago, and we've run into each other at auditions from time to time.'

'Quite a coincidence your meeting here, though.'

'Yes, I suppose so, but there aren't that many dancers around, so we all tend to know each other.'

Mack took her to the bar when the music finished, gave her a drink, and left her to get up to date on all the news with Tina. It took a while, and Tony, Pete and Ken came over, impatient to dance and be introduced. 'These are my shipmates,' Zara told Tina.

'You really are working on a ship? I can hardly believe it!' Tina exclaimed.

'Why don't you come over to the harbour and we'll show you round? Bring some of your friends along,' Pete invited expansively.

'Some of the other dancers? Do you want to meet them?'

A buffet had been laid out in a room off the ballroom. Tina led them there and soon their group had grown as she introduced them not only to some other girls but also to several of the technicians working on the film. They stood around, eating and talking, Tina letting the crew members wait on her and flirting with them a little.

Then Thor walked into the room and stood in the doorway looking round. Zara saw Tina notice him and her eyes widen, then the other girl gave a wonderful smile as she saw Thor walk towards her. The smile slipped a little when Thor said, 'Excuse me,' and turned to Tony and Pete. 'Time you two were getting back to the ship to take over the watch. Take a taxi and tell Steve and Arne to come here in it.'

'Aye, aye, Skipper.'

They obeyed him willingly but regretfully, repeating their invitation to Tina and the other girls to come and visit the ship.

Thor raised his eyebrows, but before he could turn away Tina said, 'Zara, aren't you going to introduce me?'

'Of course. This is Thor Cameron, the captain of *Spirit of the Wind*. Skipper, this is an old friend of mine, Tina Tremaine.'

'Well, hello.' Tina gave him a brilliant smile. 'I'm thrilled to meet the captain of a real sailing ship. I bet you have some thrilling sea stories to tell.'

'Not really, I——'

But Tina put a hand on his arm. 'And you look so right to be a sailor with those blue eyes and that wonderful beard.'

Thor looked taken aback. 'Thank you. If you'll excuse me, I——'

'You could tell me those sea stories while we dance,' Tina said invitingly, looking up into his eyes and smiling.

Oh, no, Zara thought with an inward groan, now he'll think that all dancers make a pass the moment they see a man they fancy.

But Thor stunned her by saying firmly, 'I'm sorry, but I think it's time I danced with Zara.' He lifted his hand in an invitational gesture towards her. 'Shall we?'

Even knowing it was just an excuse to get away from Tina, Zara couldn't resist. She smiled at the other girl. 'Come and see us on the ship. Lovely to meet you again.' And she let Thor escort her out of the room.

There were a lot of people dancing now: local Greek dignitaries with their olive-skinned dark-haired wives; actresses, make-up girls and hairdressers looking bored or animated, depending on who they were dancing with; actors with their latest beautiful, glossy girlfriends. Thor and she wouldn't be noticed, whether they danced or not. Turning to him, Zara said, 'It's OK, I know you didn't really want to dance.'

In her high heels she was much taller than usual; Thor had to adjust the direction of his eyes. 'You're mistaken,' he said on a strange note. 'I do want to dance.'

'Oh.' She could find nothing else to say, and stood there, feeling suddenly weak at the knees.

Putting a hand under her elbow, Thor led her on to the dance-floor. The gods must have taken pity on her for once, because it was a slow number. Thor put his arm round her waist and she let her left hand slip up to his shoulder. He held her lightly, at a distance, and Zara was careful to keep her hand loose in his. Her eyes were level with his mouth now and she kept her eyes fixed there, afraid to look in his eyes. Thor's top lip was thin and firm, the bottom one fuller and would probably have looked sexy if it hadn't been for the beard. She was glad he didn't have a moustache to go with the beard; she didn't like moustaches. Zara tried to picture what he would look like without the beard, anything to take her mind off his closeness and the crazy tumult of her heart.

Another couple came near to them and Thor pulled her a little closer, out of the way. Their bodies touched and she felt a scorching surge of longing that sent a violent tremor through her whole body. Desperate to cover it, unable to think, Zara said, 'I hope Tina didn't——'

'Who was your friend?' Thor said at the same time.

Moving away again, Zara somehow managed to pull herself together. 'She isn't really a friend, just someone I was in a show with some years ago.'

'She seemed—very friendly,' Thor said with irony. He looked down at her and his face didn't soften as he said, 'You look very—feminine tonight.'

Not knowing how to take that, Zara said, 'Is that good or bad?'

A fleeting smile touched his eyes. 'It's just very different. Not how you look on the ship in your shorts and top, not how you looked in your costumes when you were dancing in the nightclub back in Oran. A different Zara. One I don't recognise.'

'No, but then you don't know me very well, do you?'

His brows flickered at that. 'Perhaps not.'

'Perhaps you've even jumped to the wrong conclusions about me,' she ventured.

But that was going too far. 'I doubt it,' he said drily. 'You and your friend seem to be—very similar,' he said sarcastically.

Zara stepped back and pushed him away. Her grey eyes flamed angrily. 'That isn't fair, and you know it. You know even less about Tina than you do about me.'

'She made it very clear what kind of woman she is,' Thor retorted.

'No, she just made it clear that she found you attractive and wanted to get to know you better. Is that a crime? Don't be so damn old-fashioned. If a girl likes a man nowadays it's perfectly acceptable for her to let him know it. After all, men have been doing just that for a couple of thousand years,' she added acidly.

Thor gave her a startled look, then became aware that people were looking at them as they stood in the middle of the dance-floor. Taking her arm, he led her to one side. 'Are you saying that you would do the same, that you approve of what she did?'

She looked at him, chin high, anger in her eyes, but then lowered her head and shook it. 'No. Not the way she did it. It was too—obvious.'

'Well, I'm glad we agree about that. If you compare her behaviour to that of a man would you have danced with a man who was that—insincere, that suggestive?'

Her lips twisting into a small smile, Zara shook her head and said, 'No—I danced with you instead.'

His eyes came quickly to meet hers at that. For a moment she thought he was going to smile, but then he gave an impatient gesture. 'I've had enough of this party; I'm going back to the ship. Stay here with the others as long as you want.' With a curt nod, he walked away.

The party had gone sour with his leaving. Zara made her way out on to a terrace that overlooked the garden and found that she preferred the pounding of the waves on the nearby shore to the beat of the electric instruments the band were playing. The grounds of the hotel were guarded by a high perimeter fence. Beyond it was a road lit by an occasional street-light, and beyond that the beach and the sea. Zara had a strange feeling of the world's being divided by the fence. Within it there was the music, food, drink, and high-living of the sophisticated jet set; beyond it were the simple things of life, the wind and the sea, the sun on your face, time stretching endlessly instead of lived in a great rush, counting every minute. She felt suddenly caged by the fence and wanted to be free of it. She half turned to run out of the hotel and find her way to the beach, but suddenly stopped as she saw a tall figure in white walk across the beach and go down to the sea's edge. It was unmistakably Thor. He stood looking out to sea for several long minutes as if deep in thought, then turned abruptly and began to stride along the beach back in the direction of the harbour. He was out of sight before Zara stirred and moved out of the shadows to go back into the hotel.

Arne and Steve had arrived and were looking for her, wanting to dance, and Zara had no chance to be alone again until they left the party in the early hours of the morning. Tina and a couple of other dancers and some of the film crew were with them. 'Let's go on to a nightclub,' someone suggested. 'There's a good place called the Copacabana, where they throw plates and things.'

Everyone except Zara was enthusiastic and started whistling up taxis, but she went over to where Mack was standing with his arm around the waist of one of the hairdressers and touched his sleeve. 'I think I'll duck out, Mack, and go straight back to the ship.'

'Are you all right? Would you like me to come with you?'

'No, of course not. It's only a headache. But perhaps you could drop me off at the harbour?'

There were still a few cars and late-night tourists about as Zara got out of the taxi and waved goodbye to the others, but compared to the daytime it was very peaceful. The ramparts of the castle were floodlit, giving the ancient walls a golden glow. The sails of the medieval windmills on the harbour wall gleamed palely against the darkness of the sky. Zara had a feeling of going back in time as she walked along the quay to the wooden sailing ship. I'm getting spooky, she thought, and tried to shake off the feeling.

She could see no one on deck, but, as she climbed the gangplank and stepped aboard into the light thrown by the mainmast lamp, Thor came towards her from the shadows. He had taken off his jacket but was wearing trousers and a white short-sleeved shirt.

'Are you alone?'

'Yes. The others went on to a night-club.'

'Why didn't you go with them?'

Zara shrugged. 'I've had enough of night-clubs to last me a lifetime.' She hadn't meant to sound bitter but that was the way it came out.

Thor's brows drew into a frown. 'Did they let you come back to the ship alone?'

'No, they dropped me off at the end of the quay. I said I could come home alone the rest of the way.'

'Home? Is that how you think of the *Spirit*?' Thor asked on a surprised note.

'Why, yes, of course. Don't you?'

He didn't answer directly but said rather roughly, 'They should have seen you safely back to the ship.'

Zara walked out of the light of the lamp and looked round the deck. 'Where are Pete and Tony?'

'I let them go below. They'd had too much to drink to keep a proper watch.' She nodded, and moved towards the companion-way, but Thor said sharply, 'Don't go yet.' Then, immediately, in a stiffer tone, 'Unless you're tired, of course.'

'No, I'm not tired.' Slowly she turned to face him.

Thor's eyes were fixed on her face and he seemed to be struggling with himself, then he burst out, 'I just don't understand you.'

Zara took an unsteady breath. 'Do you want to?'

'Yes,' he said after a long moment. 'Yes, I think I do.'

'Have you changed your mind about me, then?'

'I'm constantly changing my mind about you,' he admitted on a note of self-accusation. 'As soon as I decide what kind of person you are you do something that alters my whole way of thinking.'

'Does that—bother you?' Zara moved a little nearer, her hand on the rail, her bare shoulders caressed by the soft glow of the lamp.

'Yes, it bothers me,' he said harshly. 'I don't like to be wrong about people. When you first asked for a passage on this ship I thought you were a tramp. Your using Tony to smuggle you aboard and having him in your cabin only increased that opinion. But the way you behaved afterwards, the way you look, your freshness, and your courage in the storm...' He shook his head and put up a hand to grip a rigging rope. 'I began to like you, respect you, even. I thought I'd been wrong about you, that I'd done you a great injustice.' He paused, then, his voice rough, said, 'God help me, I even began to care about you. That was something I'd vowed I'd never do again—care about a woman. In the past——' He broke off and shook his head. 'But that doesn't matter. I began to think that perhaps, in time...' He gave a raw laugh. 'But then you made it plain that you were available here and now. It was such an—an affront to what I'd begun to hope. I was convinced that you were the tramp I'd thought you, and that made me— very angry. So much so that I needed to take the anger out on you.'

'The punishment certainly didn't seem to fit the crime,' Zara agreed.

'It was the way you stood it, took all that I threw at you without a word of complaint, even though your poor hands must have become unbearably painful, that made me start to think I was wrong about you all over again.'

'And now?' Zara said softly, hardly daring to hope.

To her intense disappointment he shook his head, but then said brusquely, 'I wish you had been the tramp I first thought you. I wish I could despise you and still want you to leave the ship at the first opportunity.'

'But why? Because it's easier to hate me, is that it?' she demanded on a raw note.

'Yes. Yes, it would be very much easier.' Thor stared at her, his face set, then reached out and put a hand on her shoulder. 'But I can't. You looked so lovely tonight. And when we were dancing, when I touched you...' A tremor ran through him and his voice grew thick, ragged. 'I want you, Zara. I've wanted you ever since the storm. I've tried to fight it, but it's like a constant ache deep inside me, like a smouldering fire that won't go out.' His hand tightened on her shoulder for a moment but then he abruptly let her go.

'You tried to fight it?' Zara questioned. 'Because you thought I was a tramp?'

'Partly that. Partly because I realised that all my hopes were stupid and impossible.'

'But why? Why are they impossible?' Zara hesitated, then said, 'Thor, do you have a girl somewhere, a fiancée? Is that who writes to you from Denmark?'

'No, that's my aunt.' He didn't ask how she knew, only, 'Why do you ask?'

'I thought that perhaps you might be angry with yourself because you'd betrayed someone's trust by wanting me.'

He shook his head. 'No, it's my own trust I betrayed, my own decision never to become involved again. Because a ship is no place for a woman, and because the sea will always be part of my life.' He made an angry, dismissive gesture. 'It doesn't matter. I suppose all this is just a way of saying that I'm sorry for the way I treated you. I lost all my sense of proportion and fairness. I took my anger at myself out on you.'

'Yes, I know. I understood *that*.' Zara looked at his bleak face, made thinner and angular in the shadowed light. 'So where does that leave us?'

'I don't know.' He gave a small shrug.

'You must have had some reason for telling me all this.'

'To apologise.'

'And to tell me that you want me?'

His eyes, dark with hunger, met hers. 'Yes.'

Zara sighed, then gave a bitter little laugh. 'I can't win, can I? If I say no you'll think I'm just punishing you in turn, and if I say yes you'll be sure that I am a tramp after all.' He went to speak but she held up her hand. 'And do you seriously think that I'd run the risk of—of doing what you want and then have you turn on me again as if I were dirt? *No way.* I have some little pride left, even if I have nothing else.'

Thor tensed, straightened up. 'I deserved that. I expected nothing less.'

A flare of anger lit Zara's eyes. 'No, you didn't; you expected me to fall into your arms. You're a man, aren't you? They all think they're irresistible.'

To her surprise, he laughed. 'That sounds like the Zara I used to know, who stood up to me and told me to go to hell, more than once.' His face changed. 'It was when you didn't fight back that I began to realise that I'd hurt you, and if I could hurt you then perhaps you cared about me a little. So when I said that I wanted you— yes, I did hope that you might say yes.'

'Well, I won't,' Zara told him positively. She turned. 'I'm tired; I'm going to my cabin.'

He didn't try to stop her. 'Goodnight, Zara.'

Her cabin was hot and stuffy. Zara showered and put on her nightdress, brushed her hair and sat on her bed for a while before getting into it. The night was quiet but she didn't sleep, didn't even close her eyes. The sound of the men coming back an hour or so later carried clearly to where she lay. She heard Tony and Steve roused to go on watch again and listened as the ship grew quiet while the men slept. Getting up, she went barefoot through the darkened ship to Thor's cabin and softly opened the door. A lamp, turned very low, gave her enough light to see. He wasn't asleep. He sat up and held his hand out to her. There was no room for pride in love. Zara closed the door and went to him.

CHAPTER EIGHT

THE sun shining on her face eventually woke Zara the next morning. She stirred, wondering why she felt so languorous, so replete, and then remembered. Opening her eyes quickly, she looked for Thor, but saw that she was back in her own cabin. How she'd got there was a bit vague; she'd an idea that Thor had carried her, just as the dawn was breaking, but the rest of the night, those few hours in between, were part of her life now, something that she would remember always. With wonder, with joy.

Rolling on to her back, Zara gazed up at the cabin ceiling, experiencing in her memory those passionate hours she had spent in his arms. Their closeness had awakened a sexual fervour in each other that had taken them both by surprise. The earth would certainly have moved even if they hadn't been on a boat, Zara thought with a happy, cat-that-got-the-cream smile. She lay for a while, not wanting to break the spell, but gradually sounds drifted into her consciousness: a ferry-boat sounding its siren as it entered the harbour, the metallic clang of a crane. There were sounds on the ship, too; someone was whistling in the galley, and there were thuds and shouts on deck, as if some cargo was being loaded aboard. I ought to get up, she mused, but only the thought of seeing Thor again was sufficient lure to get her out of bed.

She showered and put on her usual shorts and sun-top, but took extra care with her hair, leaving it loose,

and put on a little make-up. I mustn't disillusion him
too quickly, she thought with the supreme confidence
that a night in Thor's arms had given her. But when she
went up on deck she found Mack in charge.

Going over to him, she gave him a beaming smile.
'Good morning.'

'You look as if your headache is better.'

Zara laughed. 'You look as if you've got one instead.'

He nodded, but as if his head was too heavy to lift.
'It developed into quite a party after you left.'

She looked round. Tony and Steve were manhandling
a drum of engine-oil aboard, but there was no one else
on deck. 'Where are the others?' she asked, only really
interested in one name.

'Most of them are sleeping it off.'

Her cheeks flushed a little. 'Even Thor?'

'Oh, no, not the skipper. He went ashore a couple of
hours ago.' Mack glanced at his watch. 'I think I'll go
and rout out Arne to take over.'

'Can I get you anything? Some breakfast?'

He gave a shudder. 'Breakfast is the last thing my
stomach wants to know about this morning.'

Most of the others felt the same way, so Zara spent
the rest of the morning on deck, ostensibly reading a
book, but in a position where she could keep an eye
open for a tall figure walking along the quay. She was
eager to see Thor again but felt strangely nervous, shy
almost. Everything had changed now—they had become
as close as a man and woman ever could be. Life opened
up before her with the rosy glow of happy anticipation,
a whole different world to yesterday.

The sun rose higher in the sky and it became too hot
to sit on deck without a shade. Reluctantly Zara went
below to make lunch, and she was down in the galley

when Thor finally returned. She heard his voice first, speaking to Arne as they came into the saloon. Tony was in the galley with her, and Ken was getting beers from the fridge. She was busy and there were people in the way, so the precious moment she had looked forward to when their eyes met again, full of the knowledge of their new relationship, became just a brief glance before Thor took his place at the table.

'I've received the instructions for the first week of shooting,' he told them. 'The film crew will come aboard early tomorrow morning and we're to sail to the island of Symi, where they've built a mock-up of the medieval harbour.'

'Why build a mock-up when they've got the real thing here?' Mack queried.

'No traffic, no gawping tourists, and no noise,' Thor said succinctly. 'We'll probably sail back tomorrow evening, but there's a possibility that we might stay overnight.' Thor looked at Zara, his face giving nothing away. 'So if we need any fresh provisions, Zara, you'll have to get them today. And would you check that the spare accommodation is clean and ready for use?'

'Aye, aye, Skipper.'

It was as mundane as that, their first exchange of words since they had become lovers. Zara gave an inward smile at the unromanticism of reality compared to dreams. Ah, well, tonight would soon come and they would be together again, lying close in Thor's narrow bed. Her eyes came up, seeking his, but Thor was talking to Mack, discussing tides and course.

She was kept busy that afternoon, cleaning out the spare accommodation. There were bunks for another twenty people divided between two areas in the bow and in the stern. These were left over from when the ship had been used as a sail-training vessel and had been kept for just such a need as this. It was shady below decks and the water outside kept the ship cool, so it wasn't unpleasant working there, but Zara was impatient to be up on deck again and finished the task as quickly as she could. Then she made out a list of fruit and vegetables and went in search of Thor for the money to go and buy them at the market. But even then there was no chance to be alone with him because some members of the film crew had arrived and he was having drinks with them in his cabin. He merely handed over the money with a brief nod, their eyes meeting for only a fleeting second, and then she had to leave in annoyed frustration. But there was always tonight to look forward to.

Two of the film crew stayed to dinner that evening, and sang for their supper by telling outrageous stories about other films they'd worked on, anecdotes of famous actors, and jokes that became so lewd that Zara took herself into the galley out of earshot. At ten o'clock, impatient to be with Thor, she left the galley, passing through the saloon. The air was heavy with cigarette smoke and smelt of beer, and it looked as if the men from the film company were set to stay for hours yet. Her eyes went to Thor and he lifted his head in an upward gesture, indicating that she go on deck.

He joined her a few minutes later. Zara would have liked to run into his arms, but couldn't because Arne and Ken were leaning against the bow rail, talking desultorily while they were on watch. They glanced round as Thor came on deck but he made a dismissive gesture and walked over to Zara, who was waiting in the shadow of the mizen-mast in the stern.

She gave a small laugh of relief as he came up to her and reached out to take his hand. 'At last! I've been longing to be alone with you all day.'

'We're not alone now,' he warned. But he lifted her hand to his lips and kissed her fingers.

Zara laughed shakily. 'Your cabin or mine tonight?' she asked in a voice already husky with anticipation.

Thor straightened up. 'Neither. I'm putting you ashore.'

She frowned, not taking it in. 'What do you mean?'

'I want you to go and pack your things. I've found a place for you to stay in the town.'

'But why?' Her voice rose in puzzled dismay.

Putting his hand on her arm, Thor drew her further away from the men in the bow. 'I should have thought that was obvious.'

'Well, it isn't to me. Why do you want me to leave now that we've—found each other?'

'For that reason. Zara, don't you understand? I don't allow the men to bring women aboard this ship, so I can't break my own rules for my own benefit.'

'But I'm already on the ship. And, besides, we could—we could keep it a secret, if that's what you want.'

He laughed sardonically. 'Have you ever tried to keep a secret aboard a ship? It's impossible in such confined quarters. If the crew hadn't been dead on their feet last night they would probably have known already.'

Her chin came up. 'I'm not afraid of their knowing. There was nothing shameful in it. Not for me, anyway.'

There was both challenge and entreaty in her voice. Recognising it, Thor lifted a long finger and gently explored her lips. 'Nor for me. But ships' captains set rules, not break them. And I'm damned if I'm going to have the men catching us sneaking from one cabin to the other.'

'So I'm to go ashore.'

'Yes.'

'And will you—visit me there?'

'That's the general idea.'

'Then the crew will know anyway.'

'Yes, but at least we'll be conducting the affair with some dignity and discretion.'

Zara wasn't sure she liked the word 'affair'. 'But my work on the ship? And I've signed up with the film company.'

'You don't have to work now if you don't want to.'

She liked that inference even less. 'I do want to.'

'Then it won't make any difference; you can join the ship every morning and work as before.'

'It all seems rather silly. And I've—I've come to like being on the ship. I feel at home here.'

'I'm sorry, Zara, but that's the way it has to be—if you want us to go on being together.'

'You know I do,' she answered forcefully. 'How can you even ask?'

'Good.' Thor leant forward and kissed her lightly. 'That's what I was hoping you'd say. Why don't you go and get your things and I'll take you ashore?'

'Will you be staying?'

He gave a sudden boyish grin that made him look as young as Tony. 'Try and keep me away.'

'What will you tell the others?'

'Just that I'll be spending the night ashore.'

'They'll guess.'

'You said you didn't care.'

'I don't. But what about you? They'll still talk about us.'

'Yes, but I won't be pulling rank to break my own rules. I won't lose their respect.' He grinned again. 'They'll probably be extremely jealous. And there are, of course, other advantages.'

There was a note of suggestiveness in his voice that made her tilt her head to one side and give him an old-fashioned look. 'Oh? And just what are those?'

He put a familiar, possessive hand on her waist. 'There will be much more privacy—and the bed is a lot bigger.'

She laughed, completely happy again. 'I rather liked your bed.'

'It cramps my style.'

'I hadn't noticed.'

Leaning forward, he said in her ear, 'Lady, you ain't seen nothing yet.'

His voice had thickened and she gave a little gasp, her own desire rising. 'I can't wait.'

'Nor can I, so why don't you go and get your things? I'm going to break up that group in the saloon or they'll be there all night. See you back here in ten minutes.'

It didn't take her that long to pack, but Zara waited until she'd heard the film men leaving and the crew hastening to their cabins to sleep off a second night of partying before she went on deck again. Thor was waiting; he had put on civilian clothes—jeans and a navy-blue sweater. Taking her bag from her, he turned to Arne. 'I'm taking Zara ashore. She'll be living in the town in future.'

'Aye, aye, Skipper,' Arne said in surprise.

'And I have business in town that will keep me there till morning,' Thor added in a voice that dared anyone to question him.

'Blimey!' Ken exclaimed, but Arne, better trained, merely nodded.

The room he'd found for her was only a short walk
from the harbour, in the old town behind the fortress
walls, and it wasn't just a room but a small flat with a
bathroom and a tiny sitting-room that overlooked a quiet
open square where an old Turkish fountain still played.
The flat was reached by an outside stair with plant-pots
full of flowers set on every step, but it was too dark to
see what colour they were. Thor had been given a large
iron key for the door and switched on the light so that
she could see her way in. She hardly looked at the sitting-
room. Thor dropped the bag on the floor, picked her
up and shouldered open the door into the bedroom. He
was right: it was a much bigger bed. And he was right,
too, about the smaller bed cramping his style.

Perhaps because that first savage urgency was over,
perhaps because they knew that they had the whole night
and didn't have to stifle their voices, their lovemaking
took on a new dimension. They undressed each other
slowly, exploringly, stroking, kissing, until Zara moaned
with longing, her body on fire. Thor laid her on the bed,
but caressed her again, driving her to a frenzied agony
of erotic desire before he took her, holding back his own
gratification to bring her to the height of sexual excitement. To Zara it was almost as if he played her like
an instrument, starting slowly and working up to a great
crescendo, but hovering on the brink, then drawing back
several times before he finally let her reach that long
plateau of overwhelming ecstasy that made her cry out
loud with rapturous pleasure. Only then did Thor give
way to his own tide of surging, thrusting passion and
let his own groan of excitement mingle with hers.

They slept then, as they had not done last night, their
bodies entwined. Zara woke first and found the light
still on. She sat up, welcoming the opportunity to look

her fill at her lover without his knowing. He was so big and strong, his muscles so powerful; it was amazing that he could be so gentle, that he didn't smother or crush her when he made love. He was beautiful, she decided. Perfect. And she smiled to herself, knowing that she only had to touch and caress him to arouse him into hungry need for her again. It was a heady power, but only because she loved him, although she hadn't told him that yet. At least, she didn't think so; she wasn't at all sure what she'd said during the abandoned transports of sexual fulfilment. But Thor hadn't said that he loved her, not yet—that she was sure of.

Her hand hovered over him, fingers spread, tempted to touch, but holding back. How different he looked in sleep, when he wasn't aroused. A great surge of intense love filled Zara's heart; she wanted to hold him close, she wanted to take care of him, be everything to him and him everything to her. She wanted to be with him always, till the day she died. Silly tears came into her eyes but she blinked them angrily away. She was getting mawkish and that wouldn't do. Deliberately she dropped her hand and began to caress him.

He came awake with a gasp, saw the dark flame of hunger in her eyes and in her parted lips, then lay back and let her do what she wanted.

Thor woke her with a kiss in the morning, but he was fully dressed. 'I have to get back to the ship; the film crew will start arriving shortly. But don't worry, we won't be sailing until eight.'

'What time is it now?'

'Five-thirty.'

She groaned. 'Do you *have* to go yet?'

'You know I do.'

'Don't sea-captains ever get holidays?'

'Maybe we can have a few days when the filming's finished.'

Putting her arms round his neck, Zara kissed him and tried to pull him back on the bed. He laughed, resisting her and yet enjoying being teased. 'Stay for just another ten minutes,' she begged.

'Zara, I—— Hey, stop that. Why, you little minx, I've a good mind to——' But somehow he dragged himself away.

After he'd gone Zara dozed a little, but then got up and showered and dressed. She found that she was terribly hungry, but of course there was nothing to eat at the flat. The morning started early in Rhodes, and there were people about as she let herself out. The flowers were red geraniums that cascaded down the staircase. Putting the key in her pocket, Zara walked through the town towards the harbour. She wore the sundress with the swirling skirt, and people smiled when they saw her radiantly happy face.

But the happiness gave way to a little frown of anxiety when she neared the ship. By now the whole crew would know that she and Thor were lovers. Zara didn't mind their knowing, but she was apprehensive of how they might take it. They were her shipmates, and, apart from the first night when Tony had got drunk, they had always treated her as one of themselves; sex had never reared its head, so to speak. But now they might look at her with new eyes, might treat her differently. Deciding that behaving just the same as always towards them would be the best course, Zara turned on to the quay.

She needn't have worried; a couple of vans were drawn up near the ship and masses of equipment were being loaded aboard. All the crew were busily helping and had no time other than to say good morning to her as they

helped the film crew stow lights, cameras, cables, and
all the other paraphernalia necessary to shoot an epi-
sode of a film. Thor was up in the bow, directing the
men, and hardly noticed her as she came aboard. Zara
slipped past them to the galley and began to sing as she
made breakfast.

They didn't finish filming that day, so spent the night
anchored off Symi. The women in the crew were given
bunks in the forward accommodation and the men aft.
If there was any sneaking around in the night it wasn't
done by Thor; he stayed firmly in his cabin as Zara had
known he would. But when they went back to Rhodes
he spent every night they were in port with her in their
tiny flat in the old town. The crew made little comment,
not to Zara anyway, although Mack did say wryly, 'It's
about time,' which completely surprised her.

It was the happiest time of Zara's life, and because
she was happy she wanted everyone else to be happy,
too. So, when Mack took her aside one day and told her
Steve's birthday was coming up, she decided it was an
excuse for a party. 'We can ask the dancers from the
film. And we'll need some music,' she said enthusi-
astically. 'Perhaps we could get a musician to come
along.'

'I was only thinking along the lines of a birthday cake,'
Mack laughed.

'Nonsense, we must celebrate properly.'

'You'd better ask the skipper first,' Mack warned.

Zara laughed, knowing that Thor wouldn't refuse her
such a simple request. And he didn't—but then he was
in no position to refuse her anything at the moment she
chose to ask him.

The party grew; from being the crew, a few girls and
a musician it became most of the film crew, a five-piece

band, and a load of hangers-on. Zara and two of the dancers worked on the cockney number she used to dance at the night-club, the wardrobe department ran up costumes for them, and they performed the routine on the deck of the ship to thunderous applause. For their own amusement they had also worked out an entirely new futuristic routine, almost a ballet, for which they wore body-stockings that extended over their heads and which were sewn with gold and silver sequins in a flowing pattern that emphasised the movements of their limbs and heads. They performed that dance, too, but later, when the party wasn't so lively.

'You were great!' People came up to congratulate them, and Steve gave Zara a sloppy kiss. 'It's the best party I've ever had,' he said in maudlin drunkenness.

Zara went down to her old cabin to change, half expecting Thor to join her there, but he didn't so she went back on deck to look for him. The party was still going on, the guests reluctant to leave, but were being gently chivvied towards the quay and waiting taxis by Thor and Arne. Thor gave her an abstracted look. 'Why don't you go ahead to the flat? I can't leave until the rest of them go and I see the ship safe.'

'All right. See you soon.'

Zara got a lift in one of the taxis and had fallen asleep by the time Thor came. She snuggled up to him as he got into bed beside her. He kissed her lightly but made no attempt to make love, instead lying back on the pillow.

'Are you tired?' she murmured.

His arm tightened round her but he didn't answer, and Zara fell asleep again, too tired to puzzle it out. He had gone when she woke up, although they weren't due to take the ship out that day. Taking her time, Zara showered and dressed, putting on a new culotte outfit that Thor had bought her. She smiled, remembering a small argument they'd had over money. 'I ought to pay my share of the rent,' she'd said guiltily.

'Don't be utterly ridiculous,' Thor had said, pulling her on to his lap.

'Well, that's a relief, because I don't have any money.'

'What happened to the wages I gave you?'

'I spent them all on the coral dress.'

He'd laughed and pulled her close. 'It was definitely worth it.'

Now, when she sauntered along to the ship, stopping to buy fruit on the way, the crew greeted her with enthusiastic gratitude for the party. She had grown so fond of them all; it was like being a member of a big family, having lots of brothers. Her eyes went to Thor; and one lover, she thought. She would very much have liked it to be one husband, but Thor had never mentioned that, either, and she was too happy to bother about the future. As far as she was concerned the here and now could go on forever.

But later that day fate, as it had a habit of doing where she was concerned, made her confront the future whether she wanted to or not. The two girls that she'd done the dance routine with arrived at the ship to collect their costumes, their voices excited as they came to find her in the saloon where she was having a cup of coffee with Thor and some of the others.

'Zara, we've got a great piece of news for you. Two things, really. You know Jonathan, the choreographer on the film? Well, he was at the party last night and he loved our new dance routine.'

'Yes,' the other chimed in. 'In fact, he's offered to help us with it, and says that if we keep together after

the film he'll also help us to get work. Isn't that
fantastic?'

'Why, yes,' Zara said in surprise. 'But——'

'And that's not all. He's offered you a part as a dancer
in the film. It will only be for about three weeks but it
will be far more money than you're getting now.'

'That's very kind of him,' Zara told them, 'but really
I'm quite happy on the ship. And as for working with
you after the film, I'm sorry, but I——'

She was about to shake her head when Thor said, 'I
think you ought to take the part in the film, Zara. The
extra money will be useful when the film's over.'

She gave him a doubtful look, finding his voice and
manner strange. 'Do you think so?'

'Yes.' He paused, then added deliberately, 'And the
three of you were good last night; it might be a good
idea to work together when you go back to England.'

Zara grew very still. Somehow she managed to smile
at the girls. 'Thanks for coming to tell me. Can I let you
know?' She got to her feet. 'Excuse me a minute.
Skipper, can I have a word with you about—about the
provisions?'

She went on deck and turned on Thor as he joined
her. 'Just what did you mean back there?'

'I wanted you to keep your options open. You'll need
work when you go home.'

She stared at him, fear catching at her heart.
'Wherever you are is home.'

His lips tightened into the stubborn line she'd come
to recognise. 'You know how I feel about women and
ships, Zara. When we leave here you won't be sailing
with us.'

'Don't you care about me?'

'You know I do,' he said shortly.

'Then what the hell is this about? You must take me with you.'

'I won't have my mistress on the ship.'

She flinched at that title. 'What about wives—are they allowed aboard?'

Putting his hands on her shoulders, Thor looked at her earnestly. 'A ship is no place for a woman. And marriage to a sailor is no life for a woman either.'

'Why not, for heaven's sake?'

'Because the men are away at sea for months on end. Because they never see their children. Because the wives have to take over running the family and become independent.' His face hardened. 'Because sailors love the sea more than their wives.'

Zara's face had become very pale. 'You're making excuses. I've always known that there was something in your life that put you off women; I think I have a right to know what it was.'

Thor let her go and straightened up. For a moment she thought he wasn't going to tell her, but then he shrugged. 'All right. I had a girlfriend when I was young, when I was just an ordinary sailor. I used to see her whenever I was home. Sailors don't earn much and she promised to wait for me until I could afford to get married. Instead she married a nine-to-five man.'

'And that put you off women?' Zara asked incredulously.

Thor shook his head. 'No, only for a while. Some years ago the ship I was on was owned by a group of men. One of them had a daughter and I fell in love with her, deeply in love. She persuaded her father to let her come with me on my next voyage. It was my first command. To some women,' he said shortly, 'being at sea seems to release all their inhibitions. Or maybe I only thought she had them. Being the only woman on the ship certainly seemed to act like an aphrodisiac on her; none of the crew was safe. She even started bringing men on board when we were in port. In the end I kicked her off the ship. She, of course, played the innocent and complained to her father, so that I lost my job. There are very few sailing ships left; once that happened it was very difficult to get taken on by any other company. When I did I vowed that there would never be another woman in my life.'

There was anger and bitterness still in his voice, and Zara could only guess at the years of hard work and striving that had enabled him to get over that first great set-back in his career. And it explained so much; why he, who was so supremely self-confident in everything else, should be so vulnerable where committing himself to a woman was concerned.

'I'm not her, Thor, I'm *me*. Surely by now you know that I love you, that I never want to leave you?'

Their eyes linked and she tried to let the love in hers convince him of her sincerity, but she knew that she'd lost when he quickly looked away again. 'It wouldn't be fair to you. You have a chance to further your career with the other girls; you should take it. You've always wanted to be a dancer.'

'No, it's what my mother always wanted. I would be perfectly contented to spend my life with you on this ship.'

'It's no place for a woman,' he repeated stubbornly.

'Won't you at least give it a chance—give me a chance? Don't you owe that much to what we've become to each other?' His face set into a stony mask of refusal. Becoming angry, Zara said bitterly, 'Damn you, Thor, you don't deserve me,' and swung away to run down the gangplank and on to the quay, too proud to let him see her cry.

Life had often gone sour on Zara before, but never as badly as this. That night she went to the flat and didn't lock the door, hoping that Thor would come and they could be together, that they could have this wonderful sexual relationship if nothing else. She lay awake most of the night, waiting, but he didn't come. She supposed the big fool would think that unfair now, too. Or else that she would have locked him out. Zara wanted to be with Thor more than anything else in the world, but she could find no way to fight his stubbornness, his disillusion with women. If loving him and giving herself to him so willingly couldn't convince him, then she just couldn't see what could. And she not only had to fight his refusal to commit himself but also his love of the sea, a love that she knew would always come first in his life. Against that she could never win. The next day she told the choreographer that she'd take the part of the dancer in the film.

The routine didn't take long to learn, and then Zara went to the ship. It took some courage to tell everyone that she was leaving and to say goodbye to them all. She gave each of them a big hug and tried hard not to cry. They looked at her with puzzled compassion, and, as they guessed what had happened, there were several angry looks for Thor when she went up to where he stood alone in the stern.

'I'd like to keep the flat on till the end of the film, if that's OK with you. Unless you want to take someone else there, of course,' she added painfully.

'Don't be silly,' he answered curtly.

She raised dark-shadowed eyes to meet his. 'The door will always be open if you change your mind.'

His face paled and he bit his lip. 'I'm sorry, Zara. I want you to know that this has been the happiest time of my life.'

She didn't ask the obvious question; what was the point? Instead she just nodded and walked away.

It took her a day or two to recover, to decide that she wasn't going to let go that easily. This, she thought, is probably my last chance of happiness and I'll be darned if I'll give it up without a fight. She spent most of the time when she wasn't working on the film in trying to think of ways in which she could most convince Thor that being together could work, even at sea. Every day she climbed the harbour wall at the end of the quay and looked at the ship, with even more longing than she had when in Oran: then it had meant a way of escape; now it meant the summit of all her dreams.

All the crew members came to see her, wishing that she were back on the ship, and bringing food along so that she could cook them a meal on the tiny electric stove in the flat. She didn't actually ask how Thor was, and they didn't come right out and say it, but she got the firm impression that he was behaving like a bear with a sore head again.

She didn't see him again until almost the end of the film, when the dancers had to double as captured island women and be forced by the Saracens to the ship to be taken to Turkey and sold as slaves. Zara was just an extra, wearing the black robes that many women in the deep south of the island still wore, and came to the quay with the other women, among them one of the female stars of the film. They had several rehearsals of being driven along by the whip-cracking janissaries, and then the usual wait before they actually started shooting. It was one of those days; things went wrong and the light

was bad. The sky kept clouding over with the ominous
hint of a tropical storm. So it was much later than they'd
expected when the ship finally put to sea so that the last
shots of the lead actress being abducted from her
homeland could be taken.

The *Spirit* had to sail out of the harbour and out to
sea for a couple of miles. There was wind enough to take
them, too much wind. Zara heard Thor advising the assistant director in charge of the shooting to wait until
tomorrow. The man almost exploded. 'We're two weeks
behind schedule as it is. OK, so everyone gets a bit
seasick, but we're only going a short way out to sea. I
insist that we go on.'

Thor shrugged, as if he didn't much care. 'All right,
if that's what you want.' He turned to give his order to
untie the mooring lines and took the ship out in just the
jigger and spanker sails. The sea caught them as soon
as they were clear of the harbour, the sky becoming black
and ominous overhead. The crew in their colourful costumes ran across the crowded deck, putting on more sail,
trying to avoid the equipment all over the place and the
huddled women, who began to cry out in genuine alarm
as the deck rolled beneath their feet.

Zara began to be afraid that someone would fall overboard, but they reached the point the director wanted
and took the necessary shots. Thor ordered the helmsman
to put about and she began to think that they would get
back to harbour safely. But then the storm broke with
unexpected suddenness and ferocity, the heavens coming
alive with an ear-shattering thunderclap and great bolts
of jagged lightning.

'Get those women below,' Thor shouted as hailstones
as hard as bullets rained down on them. 'Arne, come
down,' he yelled at the second mate, up in the swaying

crow's-nest. But Arne either didn't hear, or thought he would be safer where he was rather than risk climbing down the rigging of the pitching, heaving ship.

Mack came to shepherd the frightened women below, but Zara pulled off the black shawl round her head and stood aside, exhilarated by the storm. 'Zara, what are you doing here?'

She started to shout a reply but again the lightning came from the sky like a diabolical laser-gun and hit the mainmast, tearing off the top few feet like a matchstick and pitching Arne into the sea. Zara screamed and rushed to the side. The lifebelts had been removed for authenticity while filming, but she grabbed a rope and threw it over the side and started to lash it to the rail. The next moment a figure jumped on to the rail, poised there for a moment and dived cleanly into the sea.

'Thor!' She screamed his name but nothing could bring him back.

'All hands to lower the boat,' Mack yelled. 'Zara, get out of the way.'

But she climbed in the boat with the others and it was she, standing up precariously to peer through the driving rain, who first saw the heads in the water on the swell of a wave. 'There they are, over to the right. Thor's got him. Oh, thank God.'

'Starboard, men. Get ready to pick them up.'

They were using oars, the engine virtually useless in that sea. Mack pulled Zara down and Thor didn't see her as he helped to get Arne aboard and then heaved himself into the boat. His attention then was all for Arne as they got him back on to the ship, and Zara was so overwhelmed by relief that she hardly had the strength to lift her legs and had to be ignominiously hauled aboard at the end of a rope.

They stayed at sea until the worst of the storm passed, then headed back to Rhodes under engine-power, much to the relief of their passengers, most of whom had been ill. Mack came to tell her that Arne was all right, that he'd just swallowed a lot of water. Zara nodded; she had taken off her soaking clothes and was wearing a shirt and shorts that she'd borrowed from Tony.

'Where's Thor?'

'In his cabin.'

'Thanks.' Zara strode purposefully down the corridor, her face set. Mack watched her go, his eyes intrigued.

Marching up to his door, Zara threw it open without knocking. Thor had put on dry trousers and was just about to put on another shirt. He looked round in surprised annoyance that changed to stunned astonishment when he saw her. 'Zara! What on earth——?'

'I have just about had it up to here with you,' she yelled at him furiously. 'Not only are you a complete fool who doesn't know what's good for him, but you also have to go and risk your life! Don't you know you could have been drowned out there? You could have gone in the boat with the rest of us, but no, you couldn't wait, could you? You had to do the big-hero act.'

Thor was staring at her, open-mouthed, his arms still in the shirt.

'And I'll tell you something else,' she thundered at him. 'You're small-minded. If I loved the sea as much as you do then I'd make darn sure that I owned my own ship. And you're a blind fool, too, because you can't see that it's possible to love the sea and a woman, or that a woman could love you so much that she'd take you whatever the conditions.' Zara's chin came up, her eyes flashing fire. 'I was right when I said you don't deserve me. You're not man enough for me. Keep your stupid prejudices—I hope they keep you warm in bed at night!'

Swinging round on her heel, she marched out of the cabin and found all the crew shamelessly listening in the corridor. They cheered and clapped and got in Thor's way when he tried to come after her.

'Zara, wait!'

But she strode on, carried along by righteous fury.

Thor came to the flat that night but she wasn't there, nor at the hotel, where many of the film company were starting to think of leaving. The dancers didn't know where she was. 'I imagine she's gone back to England— quite a few people who're not staying on for the hurrah party flew out this afternoon.'

'The hurrah party?'

'The big party the producers give for everybody to celebrate the end of the film. It's tomorrow evening. Will you be going?'

'I don't know. I expect the crew will.'

The ship's part in the film finished, they spent the next day finishing the repair of the mast and preparing for sea. Or at least Mack did; Thor spent the day searching the town for Zara, trying to find out if she'd already left. He came back in the early evening looking defeated, and sat down at the saloon table, where Mack thrust a mug of coffee in front of him.

'I've lost her, Mack,' he admitted. 'I can't find her anywhere.'

'Serves you damn well right,' the mate returned unfeelingly. 'We're going to the party.'

Thor reached out and gripped his wrist. 'If she's there will you promise to let me know?'

Mack looked at him, hesitated, then nodded. 'All right, if she's there. Arne's staying on board to take the watch; he doesn't feel like drinking.'

No call came to tell him Zara was at the party, and at midnight the men came back and the *Spirit of the Wind* slipped quietly out of the harbour and out to sea. Thor stood at the rail, watching the lights of the island dwindle until there was nothing left to see. Slowly he turned away and went heavily down to his cabin.

Zara was in his bed, flipping through a magazine. She glanced up as he came in. 'I was beginning to think you weren't coming.'

He stared at her, his face lighting with stunned, astonished joy. 'How long have you been here?'

'In your cabin or on the ship?'

He gave an incredulous gasp. 'You've been here all the time!'

'Of course. Where else would I go?'

Thor shut the door. 'Do you know that I've been searching the whole of Rhodes for you? I've been through hell thinking that you'd gone back to England and I'd never find you again.' He came to sit on the bed. 'And don't tell me it serves me damn well right; I've already been told that. And it's true.' Taking the magazine from her, he tossed it aside. There was a new light in his eyes, a glow of anticipation and relieved happiness. 'Do I take it that you are stowing away again?'

'I am. And I warn you that if you try to take me back to Rhodes the crew have assured me that they will mutiny on the spot.'

'Good for them.' He pulled down the sheet and found that she wasn't wearing anything. 'Will you marry a blind fool, Zara?'

'Only if we buy our own ship.'

Thor grinned. 'As a matter of fact, I'm in the process of buying this one.'

'Really?' Zara's eyes lit, but then she pretended to be offhand again. 'That settles it, then; I love this ship.'

'More than me?' His hand caressed her shoulder, his blue eyes looking quizzically into hers.

'As much as you love the sea,' she said softly, questioningly.

'Not as much as I love you, then,' Thor said with absolute certainty.

She smiled. 'So that's all right. Why don't you come to bed?'

'Yes, ma'am.' He was beside her very quickly, his arms round her.

Zara sighed with happiness and put up a hand to stroke his face. A thought occurred to her and she said, 'Thor, you remember you laughed when I made a bikini out of that flag? What did it mean?'

He chuckled. 'It reads "Welcome aboard".'

She burst out laughing, then reached up to kiss him. 'I'll take a berth under you any time, Captain.'

Which made Thor laugh so much that it was some while before he could take her at her word.

An irresistible offer from Mills & Boon

Here's a personal invitation from Mills & Boon Reader Service, to become a regular reader of Romances. To welcome you, we'd like you to have 4 books, a CUDDLY TEDDY and a special MYSTERY GIFT absolutely FREE.

Then you could look forward each month to receiving 6 brand new Romances, delivered to your door, postage and packing free! Plus our free newsletter featuring author news, competitions, special offers and much more.

This invitation comes with no strings attached. You may cancel or suspend your subscription at any time, and still keep your free books and gifts.

It's so easy. Send no money now. Simply fill in the coupon below and post it to -
Reader Service, FREEPOST, PO Box 236, Croydon, Surrey CR9 9EL.

NO STAMP REQUIRED

Free Books Coupon

Yes! Please rush me my 4 free Romances and 2 free gifts! Please also reserve me a Reader Service subscription. If I decide to subscribe I can look forward to receiving 6 brand new Romances each month for just £9.60, postage and packing free. If I choose not to subscribe I shall write to you within 10 days - I can keep the books and gifts whatever I decide. I may cancel or suspend my subscription at any time. I am over 18 years of age.

Name Mrs/Miss/Ms/Mr _____ EP18R

Address _____

_____

Postcode _____ Signature _____

The burning secrets
of a girl's first love

Mills & Boon

Next month's Romances

Each month, you can choose from a world of variety in romance with Mills & Boon. These are the new titles to look out for next month.

DISHONOURABLE PROPOSAL Jacqueline Baird

MISTAKEN ADVERSARY Penny Jordan

NOT HIS KIND OF WOMAN Roberta Leigh

GUILTY Anne Mather

DELIBERATE PROVOCATION Emma Richmond

DEAREST TRAITOR Patricia Wilson

ISLAND PARADISE Barbara McMahon

SUMMER'S ECHO Lee Stafford

MY ONLY LOVE Lee Wilkinson

RAINBOW OF LOVE Kay Gregory

CIRCLES OF DECEIT Catherine O'Connor

LOVE ISLAND Sally Heywood

THE INTRUDER Miriam Macgregor

A HEART SET FREE Nicola West

RENT-A-BRIDE LTD Emma Goldrick

STARSIGN

FORGOTTEN FIRE Joanna Mansell